LEGENDS OF GALHALLA

A SPARK IN FATE'S HAND

BY

B. C. LICHT

Dedication

To my mother, Monica: Surprise! You have two daughters now. Not a day goes by that I don't miss you. I love you.

Table of Contents

Table of Contents	4
Chapter 1: Arrived	6
Chapter 2: Tutorial	17
Chapter 3: IRL	30
Chapter 4: Disconnect	41
Chapter 5: Escort	49
Chapter 6: Freemium	59
Chapter 7: Party	67
Chapter 8: Pirated	76
Chapter 9: Fate	83
Chapter 10: Messenger	93
Chapter 11: Bonds	100
Chapter 12: Background	108
Chapter 13: LAG	116
Chapter 14: Lore	123
Chapter 15: Crash	133
Chapter 16: Respawn	140
Chapter 17: Sneak Attack	149
Chapter 18: PVP	156
Chapter 19: Escape Key	164
Chapter 20: Guild	170
Chapter 21: Love Interest	178
Chapter 22: Pickup Group	183
Chapter 23: Dungeon	190
Chapter 24: EXPloit	196
Chapter 25: AFK	202
Chapter 26: Boss Fight	210
Chapter 27: New Game Plus	222
Acknowledgments	229

Chapter 1: Arrived

"Whenever I think about the future I'm confronted with two realities: One where everything's been decided already, and one where I'm free."
-Emma Stevenson

'*Seven stops away.*' All of Emma's hard work boils down to seven little dots on her screen. Months of mowing lawns under the sweltering summer sun, countless dog-walks through squirrel-infested neighborhoods, and a harrowing expedition into the gritty chasms of the living room couch for loose change have led to this moment. Her efforts are crystallizing into the booming image of the Spartan Delivery mascot, charging from one dot to the next, shield at the ready and package in hand.

Her heartbeat quickens as she stares at the courier's delivery route. Dark, tired eyes hide behind smudged glasses and a curtain of shaggy, brown hair. Panic seeps into her with the gripping unease of stepping into a puddle with your socks on. It moves her out of her room and down the stairs. Her unkempt mane bounces like a tumbleweed on springs with every step she takes. Long fingers run restlessly over the surface of a toy that answers the question on everyone's mind: 'what if bubble wrap was immortal?'

'*Six stops away.*' The warrior-turned-courier marches forward while Emma paces up and down the front hall, passing by the cluttered chaos that is the Stevenson family photos. Mismatched picture frames stretch from the entryway table to the wall space under the stairs like a gnarled, old tree. Its branches peak just shy of the kitchen door.

Emma never got the hang of smiling for pictures, and every petal on that tree shows it. She's cocooned in boxy clothes and sharp edges that cover a body she claims little dominion over. But there are some roots, especially the earlier ones, where she's not terribly aware of the space she occupies.

As she climbs the branches, her family flies through baby photos and birthday parties. They're off running, snoring on road trips, climbing sandy beaches, laughing, smiling, and crying. Their smiles dim gradually down towards the end of the hall as their mother grows weaker and frail, accumulating years her body's yet to experience. Until she disappears entirely. Their expressions grow solemn near the threshold of the kitchen door. Dressed in black and white, Mr. Stevenson holds his two children, standing next to a portrait of Mrs. Stevenson.

When Emma reaches that photo she doubles back to where she started, until memory lane becomes more like a treadmill she can't seem to get down from.

'FIVE.'

Three bags of potting soil slam onto the doorstep of 25 Red Hill Drive as Emma's heart is pounding out of her chest. Her head is racing with possible scenarios all branching from the tiniest details. She triple-checks the address on her phone, then opens the door to make sure, against all odds, that her address hasn't changed inexplicably since last night. 'What can go wrong' and 'just how wrong those things can get' are unfortunately Emma's bread and butter. "It's just a package," she assures herself, in a voice a little deeper than the one inside her head.

She taps her collarbone to slow down her frightening freight train of thought. At first, it shows no signs of stopping, with her mind laying more and more twisting tracks before the engine's feverish pace, but then her breathing settles and the room stops spinning. Her therapist would be proud. She's so focused on keeping time that she hardly notices the footfalls descending the stairs.

'FOUR.'

"What are you doing?" A lack of inflection and feigned disinterest are the telltale signs of her sister, Claire, who stands over the banister like a small dark specter. They passed for twins when they were younger, but that was before Emma hit puberty. Now, not so much. Emma towers over her sister, despite how often she slouches.

"Nothing," Emma answers a little too fast.

"You're doing that thing you do when you're stressed." Claire mimics Emma's tapping. She carries a bundle of depression dishes under her arm, the browser history of last week's meals. Her comfy knitted sweater presses dangerously close to the remains of last night's chicken parm. Stained sleeves don't faze Claire but the dishes give Emma a new distraction to fixate on.

"I'm stressed because there aren't any spoons left in the kitchen, give me those." Emma snags the dishes from her sister and takes them to the sink. Claire follows her into the kitchen and sits down at the counter watching Emma roll up her hoodie's sleeves. Preoccupied hands work over soapy suds and stained silverware. Claire leans on her elbow, skimming over the same three apps on her phone until curiosity gets the best of her.

'THREE.'

"Is it school?" Claire blurts out.

"Why would I stress over school? It's summer, Claire-bear."

"For now." The thought of college looms over Emma like a colossal tidal wave poised to take over her. It grows taller and taller, swelling with the weight of her father's expectations, her fear of the unknown, and the eyes of thousands of students, until the wave threatens to consume all she's ever known. She'd sooner grow gills than think about it.

"I got it covered." She deflects.

"Did your therapist dump you again?"

"Not yet. We're taking things slow." Emma shakes her head as scalding hot waters erode chocolate-smeared mountains and cookie-crumbled canyons. "And for the last time, my last therapist didn't dump me. He just needs some personal time to take care of a few things."

"I can't believe you fell for the 'it's not you, it's me.'" Emma gives Claire a withering stare, threatening her with the fury of a box full of kittens.

"Is it friends? Or lack thereof?"

"Claire, I'm fine. Honestly." Emma prepares a bowl of cereal and hands it to Claire. "This one better not make it to your bedroom."

"You sound just like mom." Claire's scoff catches in her throat, cut sharp by jagged realization. Suddenly the room is quiet. "... Sorry."

"No worries. She was your mom, too," Emma forces a smile straight from the front hall and turns her attention back to scrubbing hardened, cheese barnacles off of one of the bowls.

'TWO.'

"You clean when you're nervous." Claire continues. "Every time you have a test your room looks like a Grapple store. Well, minus the smell," she says through a spoonful of cereal. "Congrats on being the only guy I know whose room doesn't smell like B.O."

"Thanks for the compliment... I guess?" Claire mulls over her cereal, swirling her spoon in the bowl as she chooses her next words carefully.

"You can talk to me, you know? About anything." Emma nearly drops the dishes, stopping cold in her tracks. Claire wouldn't be saying this if she didn't suspect something was going on and

Emma's face was always easy to read growing up. She could be offering Emma an out. As good a chance as ever to tell Claire that she's not their father's only daughter.

Then again Claire might not understand, and she can't risk losing her. Fear grips tightly around Emma's throat leaving just enough room for her to squeeze three, small words.

"We'll talk later."

"Ok." Claire stands up and takes her bowl with her upstairs, leaving Emma alone with her thoughts.

'*ONE.*'

Mr. Reyes delights in finding the costumes he ordered for the school play on his doorstep, the final stop between the courier and Emma. She dries her hands off the washcloth hanging from the oven handlebar when her phone vibrates on the counter. Its frantic dancing heralds the courier's approach. She looks down at the notification on her screen and the color drains from her face.

"Shit, I gotta sign for this." With her hood pulled up she tiptoes down the front hall towards the door. "*Deep breath, confidence. You're never going to see this person again. Deep breath... confidence...*" Footsteps creep on the other side of the door. A shadow takes shape behind the window.
"*Confidence. Confidence!*"

'ARRIVED!'

The doorbell rings. Emma swings the door open with the urgency of someone who's left a fork in the microwave. The courier stares at her with his finger still hovering over the doorbell, taken aback by her sudden movement. He's older, about her dad's age, sporting a mustache, a round belly, and skinny legs. He clears his throat, looking at his Spartan Delivery datapad.

"Morning. Package for..."

"Yes!" Emma blurts. The delivery person raises an eyebrow at her.

"I didn't say the name yet."

"You don't have to." Emma folds her arms, gritting her teeth into a smile.

"Sign here." He hands her a stylus and a pad with the grace of someone who isn't paid enough to investigate any further. He looks around the neighborhood before eyeing the package. "That's that new VR thing my son's been going on about, huh?"

"Maybe? I don't know your son."

"Yeah well, can't say I see the appeal. Too realistic if you ask me. If you want something that intense you might as well experience the real thing." His hearty chuckle shamelessly searches for approval as if it's open mic night. But Emma writes down a name that she feels little to no connection to and nods her head, absently.

"Uh-huh. Can't exactly fight giants in real life, can you? Not after Don Quixote," she says, offering the pad back to him in exchange for the package.

The courier's expression is fraught with disapproval.

"Guess so. Well… enjoy your day, sir. And your uh… goblins and ghosties," he waves his hand dismissively, heading back to his van. Emma closes the door behind her and lets out a deep breath. She leans against the door and slides down until she's sitting on the floor.

"I should have corrected him. No, what good would it do? I'm never going to see him again. So don't sweat it. He didn't know any better. He sees what everyone else sees. It's fine, everything's fine." At least that's what she tells herself. *"… But it doesn't feel fine."* None of that matters anyway, now that she has what she's been dreaming of.

Emma picks herself up and runs up the stairs to her room. She shuts the door behind her with unbridled glee, too eager to think about the breakfast she's just missed. Her room is filled with posters, each one a portal to a different world, a different sanctuary for her to hide away.

Maps depict forgotten jungles and far-off civilizations hanging side by side with star charts plotting delicate courses around starving black holes. Stealthy assassins strike from the shadows as hulking warriors rush in to protect their wizard companions. But what she took pride in most of all was a collection of unrelated game covers arranged in a subtle pattern of blues and pinks with a white stripe right down the center.

She plops down at her desk and jiggles the mouse to wake her computer. Her background blinks to life with a warrior woman raising her fists, surrounded by a hoard of mutated adversaries.

Emma opens the game launcher she prepped the night before. A wall of text fills the launcher blocking screenshots of dark caverns and ethereal seas, courtesy of the Reality Realty game company. "... Day One Patch, hotfixes? Already?" Emma shrugs, swiveling in her chair as the patch loads. "*Games have come a long way since Pickmon.*" She thinks to herself.

A few hours of webcomics and the game launches in earnest with jaunty fanfare and a cheering sound clip. Emma plugs in her headset and adjusts the visor over her eyes. The double R logo fades and her body takes flight, floating above a sky full of fluffy white clouds.

They part before her revealing the title screen: a sprawling landscape of rolling green hills and sturdy mountains dotted with lone castles and hungry caves. A wizened voice greets her and the logo appears in bold, heroic lettering.

"Welcome, hero… to Legends of Galhalla." A trio of swords swishes into place below the logo as a triumphant score plays. Emma grabs a hold of one of the swords with the words 'Create a Character' etched into the fuller. Searing bright light pours out of the letters until the sword vanishes in her hands and her vision pales. In the middle of the white nothingness stands a black stone archway covered in gold detail and a heavy blanket of moss. Mercury pours from the other side of the arch until Emma is faced with her reflection, staring back at her from the mirrored waterfall. "Now," the voice speaks, "who are you?" Emma grimaces at her image.

"Y'all just had to scan me," she cringes, immediately fiddling with the customizing sliders, working her way from the ground up. "Couldn't do with a range of presets to choose from? No, we're fancy, aren't we?" She softens her edges, rounds her corners, sanding down everything about her body she finds alien. Emma shrinks the frame down a couple of inches and grows her hair down to her shoulders.

It's still her. She still has her eyes and her freckles. Her hair is still shaggy if not longer and better maintained. The rest of it? Hopes and dreams, bits and pieces taken from her favorite heroes. In a way, it was more her than reality would ever dare allow. "This is me," she exhales.

"Now, what will you become?" Emma's eyes narrow as the wizened voice distorts slightly. A damp, stone cellar assembles itself around her new reflection, brick by brick. Aisles of barrels march into the dim light before settling down in place. Ice elementals patrol the rows, their icy hooves clip-clop noisily along the cobbled floors, chilling the wine with every step.

With a wave of her hand, the chilly goats evaporate into mist. The stones give way to lush, green forests. Towering trees stretch tirelessly into the skies. A web of rope bridges connects the trunks like man-made mycelium, suspended in the open air. Another wave and she's taken to a princess's tower, submerged in a deep, dark lake. Haunting calls fill her ears until she switches to the next background.

A wind farmer's loft clings tightly to floating islands as airships set sail with their eyes set on the horizon. Another wave and the loft shifts into a swaying sea captain's cabin filled with treasure; none of them seemed to fit her until Emma stumbles upon a modest, warm room. Sunlight peeks shyly through curtains that slowly dance in the wind's gentle caress. Her heart melts when she sees flowers on the windowsill. Orchids, her mother's favorite.

Emma clicks next and a text box materializes before her. She enters a name that she's taken with using online just as much as it was taken with her. *"Ember."* After a gentle reminder of how permanent this creation process is, she steps through the mercurial image and into the room. Ember's room. Her room.

When Ember turns around to look for the arch it's gone. In its place is a floor-length mirror reflecting her hopes and dreams. The character creator and the weight of the real world are now lifetimes behind her. She stares into her reflection and can't stop smiling.

Chapter 2: Tutorial

"Hint: Creating a character doesn't stop at character creation! Your experiences in Galhalla are just as important in shaping your hero!"
-RR

In the waking hours of the morning, outside Ember's window stirs the bustling port of Harbortown. Yawns and chatter are punctuated by the steady pounding of a blacksmith's hammer. The steeple's bell cheerfully greets the ever-present sound of waves hitting the shore. The enticing aromas of baking bread and freshly caught fish swirl lazily into the sky, only to stop and take a break at every open window. Horse-drawn carts wheel cargo up and down walkways of wooden planks suspended over gentle, lapping waters. Clinking, glittery coins change hands from captain, to quartermaster, to crew, before landing in the pockets of land-faring merchants and cooks, all in captivating detail.

A clear line cuts through Harbortown like a cleaver, separating fish head from fish tail. Old Harbortown still has dry land to stand on with traditional architecture and (allegedly) well-to-do folk. The closer you get to the shore the more experimental the architecture becomes. They're buildings are crafted from recycled pieces of shipwrecks found in the bay until you reach the water. New Harbortown is built on the hulls of docked ships too bloated to leave, trapped by an ever-expanding network of wooden walkways. Every establishment, home, and stall owes its real estate to some galley or pirate ship that's been abandoned, refurbished, and repurposed, like the newly renovated Sip & Sail, Wixley's take on an eatery and sleepery.

Underneath Ember's window hangs the tavern sign. Enchanted steam floats out of an engraved mug sitting on a napkin or a ship's sail depending on where you're standing. This rustic inn is nestled in the bones of a derelict pleasure barge right at the top of Drain Street, near spitting distance from Old Harbortown. All of it feels real, from the heat of the sun to the linens of her clothes to the salt in the air. If this is all a dream then Ember fears waking.

"If it's all the same to you, I could use some help down here!" A stern, yet teasing voice shouts from downstairs. Ember snatches an apron hanging from her bed's short post and runs downstairs into the tavern. Standing on a chair in the middle of the dining area is the barkeep and owner of the Sip & Sail, Wixley the human. "'Bout time you woke up." Their kind eyes are perched atop a generous smile and a mountain of muscle. Scars peek from the sleeves of their tunic, crisscrossing their arms. A large exclamation mark floats over their head.

"Sorry," Ember apologizes, "I got distracted,"

"I figured, a lot of the new arrivals get like that. Staring off into space while the whole world moves around them," Wixley chuckles, "… no offense."

"None taken. Why are you standing on a chair? Is the floor lava?"

"What? No, no, that was last week. This is much worse."

"Worse than lava?" Wixley nods their head and crosses their arms.

"Much worse, it's rats."

"Rats?"

"You heard me, rats! Damn critters are in the cellar, crawling all over my mead, chewing up the hull. I think I even saw one with a sword! I can't have the Sip & Sail's good name tarnished by a hoard of scurrying stowaways. I'll never hear the end of it, especially if Gale catches wind, she'll spread the word like wildfire."

"And you're on a chair because?"

"I don't like rats, alright?!?" Wixley huffed.

"Didn't you save Harbortown from a sea serpent in one of the promotional comics?" Wixley's eyes narrow on Ember,

"The fact that you heard my legend from the mouth of some sort of comedian troubles me, deeply."

"Not that kind of comic…" Ember smirks, but Wixley pushes through.

"My tale was grand and epic. I'd sooner hear a tax collector's soliloquy of my exploits than listen to some comic from the Chuckle Cove butchering -my- journey. Yes, I did save the town. From a SEA serpent. Not a hoard of rats. I draw the line at rats. Now, go grab something-... anything from under the counter, and deal with them. I'll make it worth your time." Ember arches an eyebrow.

"Anything from under the counter?"

"Yes, whatever floats your rat-killing boat," Wixley sighs, exasperated, their exclamation mark morphs into a faded question mark. With Ember's first entry chiseled into her quest log, she kneels under the counter. Her employer's aversion to rats manifested into a practical armory filled with a myriad of items fit for rat eradication, including the E-rat-icator.

"'Blur the line between broom and buzzsaw,' yeah, I'll pass." She moves over to an ornate flute. " The 'Whistle Launcher.' This is giving me serious Pied Piper vibes. Nah." Her eyes grow wide with excitement. "Oh!!! Hi there, I'm taking you with me." She bundles this calico ball of fur into her arms and shouts at Wixley from behind the bar, "you said I could pick anything under the counter, right Wixley?"

"As long as it gets the job done, I don't care-..." their face falls flat as Ember stands up, "Ember, that's a cat."

"Sure is," Ember smiles, petting her newfound friend.

"You sure you don't want the broom? This feels a bit chancy."

"Chancier than a broom that can maim me? Thanks, but I'll pass." Wixley stares at Ember who's far too busy entertaining her new, furry friend. "Chance has a nice ring to it," she says as she turns her attention back to Wixley, "doesn't it?" Chance leans into Ember's chin-scratches. "Doesn't it, Chance?"

"Touching." Wixley coughs. "Welp, those rats aren't going to ferret themselves… so." Wixley shoos them away with their hands.

"We're on it," Ember speaks for Chance, holding out her paw towards Wixley. Together the two descend the creaking steps into the cellar, formerly the ship's hold. Squeaks pierce through the dark, cold, quiet, bouncing off the floorboards. Ember places Chance down on the floor gingerly, "Alright girl, do your thing." She takes one look at Ember before ignoring her completely. Unbothered by her new owner's exuberance, Chance moves on to more pressing matters, namely a tongue bath. "Come on, kitty, go get your lunch."

"You'd have better luck catching the rodents yourself, darling. I don't do labor." Chance speaks in a rich, bold voice that stops Ember in her tracks. She returns to her bath.

"You can talk?!?"

"So can you." She quips between licks. "You don't see me making a big fuss over it."

"But, you're a cat."

"That's a little narrow-minded of you and undeserved. Even if I -was- a cat." Ember tilts her head at the cat that wasn't a cat.

"Then, what are you?"

"I'm your familiar, darling. Your living conduit to the arcane weave. As long as I'm by your side you wield your magic in the palm of your hand, like a ball of yarn. That reminds me, you're going to need some new clothes." Chance swirls her tail and Ember's apron melds into a set of wizard's robes. She marvels at the sleeves. Chance's magic managed to keep some of the finer details of her apron while embellishing them with a feline touch. "And this…" The familiar launches into a fit of dry coughs. Ember averts her eyes but when the coughing subsides she finds a dusty, leather-bound book on the floor where a hairball should be.

"Gross… Is that contagious?"

"It's your Tome, darling. You're going to need it to cast your spells and write down the more complicated ones in case you forget. Keep it close. No Tome, no spells, and most importantly, no me." Chance places the back of her paw on her forehead, dramatically. Ember lifts the book warily, flipping through the pages.

"They're all blank."

"Well, you haven't experienced anything worth casting spells from. Here, let me give you a few free samples. Can't have you smacking your adversaries around with pen and paper alone, now can we?" Chance leaps onto the book. It bounces in Ember's hands under her weight. Ink pours from her paw prints, bleeding into the pages, and swirling into words and diagrams. Chance settles around Ember's shoulders, admiring her handiwork. "We'll start you off with the basics."

"Tire Ball, Dice Shard, Detect Tragic-... Please tell me if these are all spelling errors."

"Afraid not."

"Is my Tome trapped inside another familiar? Where's the fireball? Or teleport?"

"I'll have you know these are fine spells. We all start somewhere. If you're going to bend the laws of the arcane to your will then you must learn how to poke at reality's defenses and find its weak spots. Surely you've experienced it before? Magic starts with wordplay. Every little turn of phrase contains the smallest droplets of mana. The magic in the mundane. You harness that with these," she gestures at the spells, "until you're powerful enough not to need them."

"I should've picked the Whistle Launcher." Chance hissed at her new apprentice. "Alright, alright, I'll start looking through this joke book." She flips through the pages, scowling as she pictures how much fun the magic monk who penned this work must have had. "'Small Talk: Find common ground between the caster and intended target. See eye-to-eye...' It's no fireball, but I don't wanna roast these little guys, either." Ember selects the spell, and arcane glyphs circle her fingertip as Chance's eyes glow blue. She aims it toward where she hears the most squeaking and fires away.

The room grows quiet and then the cellar grows larger, stretching itself around Ember, or perhaps Ember was shrinking. "Ahhh eye-to-eye, I get it. Real funny" She says as she hits mouse height. Ember peers into the vast expanse of a floorboard desert dotted with crumbs playing tumbleweed underneath mountains of shelves and casks. In the distance, a gathering of rats huddles amongst themselves in the far, dark corner of the room, closest to where the rudder might be. It's a harrowing journey, past gaping sinkholes in the floorboards and colossal dust bunnies, but Ember makes it close enough to hear the ensuing debate.

"Our new home is too dangerous," cries a squeaky voice in the corner. This rat wore chewed linen scraps, holding a gnarled root in one paw for support, and standing on a staircase of forgotten coins. "The giants stomp down here! They yell their great and terrible yells! The last one thundered to the overworld," the gnarled root points up to the stairs, "no doubt to bring more giants to aid! How many rats must be trampled under giant-foot before we take action? How many lives must be lost to trap and snare? We cannot stay here, we must flee!" The crowd erupts into fearful murmurs and whispers until a lone rat makes himself known.

"Terrible yells?" This cocky rat scoffs from atop a long-discarded spool wearing leafy leathers and holding a button for a buckler. He drops down and swaggers among the crowd as he speaks. "I'm sure that's what it looked like from down here, but I was scaling the mountain ranges." He points to the shelves. "I was nose-to-nose with the giant myself! I heard a scream. They -fear- us. We outnumber them! This is our home now, and this is our food! We back down now and we spend the rest of our lives fleeing from shadows that only grow longer."

"Bramble's right," a kindly rat speaks, sitting in a chair fashioned from an old peanut shell. "I know we grow tired of scraping by when the giants don't have to. Our children are too young to remember what life was like in the forests and for that I am grateful. This dark home is more than we can ask for. The skies are clear of owls. The land is clear of cats. We worked hard to escape the Tangled Wood for good reason. I will not return just so my offspring can suffer the same slights I've suffered all my years." Ember was taken aback.

"Wow, who knew rat politics could be so intense?" she wondered. The rats turn their heads in her direction. "I said that out loud... didn't I?" The collective rodent rabble backs up, clearing a wide berth around Ember.

"This rat has no fur!" The first rat points at Ember with his gnarled root, "and no tail! The horror! What have those giants done to her?"

"I don't think that's a rat, Crumble." The kindly rat adjusts their spectacles. "I think it's-"

"A GIANT!" Bramble leaps into action, unsheathing a sharpened thorn mere inches from Ember's face, "But she doesn't soar into the clouds and her words are clear to us. What business do you have here in Ratlantis? Tell us now. Before I add 'Giantslayer' to my long list of monikers." Ember eyes the thorn before looking out into the crowd.

"My boss wants me to get rid of you guys," Ember says, matter-of-factly. The rats gasp collectively, and Bramble's thorn inches ever so closer to Ember's throat. "But I don't wanna do that! I figured we could talk. I know what it's like trying to find a new home, my last home kinda felt like a dark cellar, so I can relate."

"Quit your bragging, Giant." Bramble sneers. "We are very lucky to call this dark and cozy cellar 'home.' You live in a land of endless cheese and sunflower seeds. Why should we parlay with you?"

"Well, they're not exactly endless... it just feels like that because you're all much smaller."

"We're regularly sized, you're the ones who are grotesquely huge!"

"Bramble, that is enough." The elder rat turns to Ember. "You must forgive him, Giant. He is... spirited. I'm Thimble and the one in the linens is Crumble."

"I'm Ember."

"You've caught us at a dire time, Ember. Our family stands divided over matters of safety, food, and shelter. And while some of these hardships are done by the hand of your kind, we've never had the opportunity to hear a giant's perspective. Tell us, what are your thoughts on the matter?"

"Why should we trust her?" Cried Crumble, pointing his gnarled root at Ember. "She's a giant! Surely this is some sort of trick!"

"We're the same size right now," Ember reminded him, "I think you can stop calling me a giant."

"She's still a giant, at heart," Bramble spat.

"Thanks… I think." Ember tilts the thorn away from her throat. "Look, Wixley's afraid of rats and they don't want you crawling around the food, it's a bit of a health issue."

"Health issue?" Asked Thimble. "None of us have gotten sick from the food yet."

"Right but the 'giants' could get sick from you handling the food." Bramble's face lights up as a smile curls on his face.

"Wait, you mean to tell me that we barely have to lift a claw against the giants and they'll get sick? Oh, this is glorious!"

"Yes, yes," Ember stumbles, "But they might retaliate, with cats and traps, and nobody wants that, except maybe the cats, and who knows what their politics must be like."

"A bold move to speak of cats in such a lighthearted tone. Those remarks could be your end if you're not careful, Giant." Crumble warns Ember with a shaken fist. Bramble bounces on his little toes.

"Say the word, Crumble! I've been waiting for this day!"

"What I mean is that I see your needs as well as Wixley's. We can't have you scaring my boss daily or I'll be out of a job, but that doesn't mean we have to force you out of your new home." Ember places a finger thoughtfully on her chin. "Ratlantis should stay here. Wixley'll be more accepting once I tell them you guys have your own culture and civilization. I'll make sure no harm comes to you and that you're all well fed, as long as you keep away from the food stores, and the 'mountain ranges.'"

"How can we trust you?" Bramble asks. Ember opens her mouth but her response is eclipsed by a large shadow over the whole of Ratlantis. Sharp claws scrape along the wooden floor. The glowing eyes of a furry titan are more than enough to drain the color from every face in Ratlantis, save for Bramble who faces the new threat with the grave bravery of a last stand.

"Ember darling, I'm bored." Chance whines as she towers above Ember, surveying the gathering of rats with mild disinterest as they stand frozen in fear until one rat screams.

"A cat!" Crumble stumbles off of his raised platform and into the crowd, face first. "Flee! Flee for your very lives!!!"

"Again, I'm not a cat." Chance groans at the fleeing populace.

"The great beast knows the Giant's tongue!!!" Crumble cries, shoving his way through the crowd. "We're doomed!!!"

"Chance! Get out of here!!!" Ember pleads with her familiar who rolls her eyes at the ensuing chaos. She turns on her heel and tiptoes towards the stairs. When Ember turns around she finds the rats have stopped their spirited retreat to stare at her in awe. Thimble breaks the silence.

"You command the great cat to leave us be."

"Well, 'command' is a pretty strong word, but I'll take it." Thimble clasps her paws.

"You are quite powerful, Ember of the Giants. Your words ring true. A partnership between our people would benefit us both. We accept your proposal."

Together Ember and Thimble drew up a treaty detailing the protections Ember offered, daily deliveries of food imported directly to the city of Ratlantis, and the city limits of Ratlantis. Signatures were penned beside rodent pawprints just before her new friend's words began to lose their meaning.

Ember bid them farewell in broken rat speech and they responded in crumbling human phrases. The miles-long journey to the stairwell shrunk back into steps and the mountain ranges became shelves once more. As she stands in the cellar the world feels both smaller and bigger than it did before.

Chance waited for her apprentice on the foot of the stairs, arching her back into a nice stretch upon her arrival. "Not how I would have done it, but a nice change of pace, to be sure. I suppose you've earned your fireball." The two walk up the steps and into the tavern dining room to find Wixley washing mugs behind the bar. Their question mark is now filled in with a satisfying gold.

"Oh good! You're done? Please tell me you got rid of them." Ember shakes her head as she affixes the tiny treaty to a place of prominence behind the bar.

"Nope, they're here to stay."

"You're kidding me! I knew I should have just given you the E-rat-icator." Their hand pinches the bridge of their nose.

"It's not that bad! They just need a home. They have their own culture and lives. They deserve a safe place to live just like the rest of us! As long as we keep them fed and safe you don't have to worry about them running all over your food and they don't have to worry about the Hero of Harbortown busting out the buzz-bat... Right?" Wixley eyes the bat, but ultimately thinks against it.

"Fine, fine. I guess you took care of it," they grumble, "but I'm coming after you if this deal doesn't work out. Here's your reward." They toss a small sack of coins for Ember to catch. The quest vanishes from her log and so does Wixley's question mark. Ember jumps suddenly as she feels her Tome morphing in her hand. The ragged, leather cover fizzles away into smooth, gray moleskin with tiny rats engraved into the corners. Floating words dance above her head, written in cheerful sparks.

"Achievement Unlocked: Diplorat."

Chapter 3: IRL

"Hint: Be sure to take a twenty-minute break for every sixty minutes of playtime. Your health is important and Galhalla will still be there when you return!"
 -RR

"Not bad for your first day casting spells, darling." Chance leaps onto Ember's bed, giving her side of the bed a solid kneading session before curling herself into a ball of fur. The cold night air sends a breeze through the curtains and the full moon bathes the room in a pale glow. Her apprentice dons a sleeping gown and stares at her reflection in the mirror almost as if in a trance. "Careful now, if you stare too long you'll fall in." Ember catches herself, embarrassed.

"Sorry, I'm just not used to it." Chance wrinkled her nose at that.

"Not used to it? How can you not be used to your reflection?" Ember stays quiet and Chance sighs. "Come now, it's time for bed." Ember steps a few paces before freezing still, inches away from her bed, tears welling in her eyes. Her voice is barely a whisper.

"I don't want to go back."

"I see. Everyone goes back eventually, Ember. The world you came from isn't going to disappear overnight… whatever you're running away from is merely waiting for you to confront it."

"I don't want to confront anything, Chance. I just want to live."

"Then is that really living?" Ember doesn't answer. "Don't stay up too late, darling. Tomorrow is a better day." Ember eases into bed, fighting sleep tooth and nail, her finger hovering over the logout button. But she's in bed, and whenever Emma's in bed she hears her mother's lullaby. And on nights when her anxiety wraps around her like a blanket, she sings it.

"Worry and Fright
Won't get you tonight
So long as I'm here
As long as you're near…"

In the end, she presses it, and sleep takes her away from Galhalla and back to reality. A health alert pops onto the screen suggesting she take a break from playing for a few minutes, and so she does. It's a stark disconnect, going from the vibrant hues, and the warm wood of the tavern to the baby blue walls of Emma's room. So much so that she has to rub her eyes to get readjusted. A gentle tapping knocks Emma out of her daze and into her body.

"It's dinner time," Claire spoke from behind the door, "… Dad's home." Emma's heart starts racing as stress pumps through her veins again. She debates on whether to go to bed early or play sick, but her stomach grumbles fiercely, eager to remind her of the meals she's missed. Her hand reaches up to tap her collarbone as she exhales, shakily.

"I'll be right down."

It's a long walk to the dining room table and Emma feels herself shrinking with every step, an impressive feat from six feet tall. But instead of engaging in a fair bit of diplomacy, Emma sees her father, Mr. Stevenson, unloading a chicken dinner from a take-out bag and onto the table. He places each container down with the precision and command of a four-star general inspecting his troops. The man was practically set in stone. It was almost suffocating, Emma felt like a hyena encroaching upon a lion's meal.

"W-welcome home, dad," she manages.

"Dinner's ready, son," he answers.

"How was work?" Claire asks.

"Work was work," Mr. Stevenson blusters, loading his plate up with mashed potatoes. "One of the new guys quit. He didn't even give us a two-week notice, but he made a big, showy speech so he could whine about working conditions. I'd say the factory's better off without him except my higher-ups gave me his workload." He pours gravy over his mashed potatoes while Emma stares at them intently, avoiding eye contact. She sees herself in the smothered side dish as her father's frustrations smother the conversation. "Back in the day, they'd give you the quitter's wages if you stepped up to the plate or a promotion."

"Sounds tough," Claire offered, neutral.

"It -is- tough." Mr. Stevenson bristles. "It's not enough to just have a job anymore. You have to be the boss. Both of you." He said, pointing a drumstick at Emma and Claire. "You understand?" Claire gives him a half-hearted nod, but Emma has just enough of her mother in her to let loose one, small spark.

"Why don't you look somewhere else for work?" She says, more to her mashed potatoes than anyone. A little louder than a whisper, but loud enough for her to regret it as the words leave her mouth. Her father fumes.

"It's like this everywhere. Even if there was a better place, it's far too risky changing things. I'd have to get a read on my new supervisors, I'd lose my seniority and have to change my schedule. I worked hard to get that schedule. New-hires would kill to get weekends off. I have you two I need to take care of. I can't just jump ship and hope for the best. You kids want to end up in the streets when I'm in between jobs? No? Didn't think so." Against her better judgment, Emma persists.

"What if I get a job? I could bring in some extra money. Help out."

"Absolutely not. If you get a job you'll get distracted, I've seen it hundreds of times at the factory. You'll find a girl, settle down, then twenty years down the line you'll have your own children to take care of. You don't want to end up like your old man."

"Is that so bad? As long as we're happy, what difference does it make?"

"A huge difference. You're young. You have no idea what makes you happy yet. You need to focus on your schoolwork. The same goes for you, Claire. You still want to be a vet? Well, you're not going to get there by giving biology your second best." Not a word escapes from Claire's mouth. He turns his attention back to Emma, "and you need to figure out what you want to do with your life. If you think you can just waltz through college without a care in the world then you have another thing coming." Color flushes to Emma's cheeks as her pulse vibrates throughout her body. Her voice is straining at the edge of tears.

"So we're just supposed to watch you be miserable while you steer us away from your mistakes? 'Nothing works and nothing helps' because that's just the way things are? What's the point of telling us your problems if it doesn't matter what we have to say? You don't want advice, you don't want pity, what do you want?!?" A silent storm churns behind Mr. Stevenson's forehead. He places his drumstick down, his calm and measured movements do little to mask his building temper.

"You have no idea how the real world actually works. It's so much more complicated than that. So don't get upset when I don't drop everything I'm doing, for your sake might I add, to follow your 'advice.' Especially when it can screw us all out of a roof over our heads. Yes, I am miserable, but I'm doing it so that your life is better than mine. So Claire's life is better than mine. That's how life works. You should be thanking me!" Emma ignites.

"We didn't ask you to be miserable! God! You and mom had this same fight over and over again! When are you going to wake up and do something about it?" Emma fumes, hot angry tears gather around the corners of her eyes. Claire leaves the dinner table with the grace of a ghost. Mr. Stevenson's face grows a dangerous shade of red.

"You don't get to sit there and criticize my life when you're not the one living it. I am the parent, you are the child. You can start talking to me like a man when you start acting like one. As long as you're under my roof, living off of my income, you don't get a say in how I make it or how I raise you… How dare you speak up to me like that, you should be ashamed-!"

Emma launches herself up from the dinner table and rushes up the stairs. Her dad's shouting digs into her ears as she slams her door shut and buries herself under the covers. She sobs. Harder than she's ever sobbed in a long time. Emma loses herself to her frustration, her anger, and her grief until her emotions swirl into a burning purpose. She scrolls through her phone, flipping through job listings, but each open position dulls her fiery anger until she is left with a numbing melancholy. *"Even if I did get a job it would only make things worse."* A sturdy knock rattles on her door followed by a freshly cleared throat. Her heart starts pounding again. *"I forgot to lock the door."*

"Can I come in?" Mr. Stevenson asks more out of habit than respect. Emma doesn't answer but the door opens anyway. She hears heavy footsteps approaching as she stays under the covers. Her bed springs squeak in protest as her father sits beside the shape of her. He lets loose a heavy sigh and scratches the back of his neck. "Look, I'm not going to sit here and pretend what you did was even remotely ok. Because it wasn't." His voice is still on the edge of anger, but he dials it back a few paces. "What… happened to you? You've changed. You used to be my little buddy and now you can't talk to me without getting upset. All we ever do is fight. I know losing your mother was hard, but you can't keep doing this to me. I'm doing the best I can."

Emma sees her responses laid out before her in her mind's eye like multiple choices in a dialogue tree. '*You're the one who's changed.*' That's gonna cost a dip into their relationship. '*I have not yet begun to change!*' Funny, but now might not be the best time to come out. '*I wouldn't fight with you if you listened to me every once and a while.*' Honest, too honest. No matter how many options pop up every one of them leads her down the path to another fight, so she stalls, waiting for the dialogue counter to run down.

Mr. Stevenson puts his hands on his knees and catapults himself off of her bed. He blusters, takes a final look around the room, and walks out the door, shutting it. His steps echo down the hall and Emma stops holding her breath. She hums her mother's lullaby as her hand reaches out from under the blanket, fumbling over her desk until her fingers find her VR visor. She pulls it under the covers, and turns it on, picking up where she left off.

Ember flips over the covers and is back in the Sip & Sail with Chance right where she left her. The air is still and the hour is three. She makes her way down into the tavern. It's dark, but not so dark that Ember can't find a candle to light. She pulls up a bar stool, but the pegs scrape on the wooden floor like thunder claps against the silence. "****!!" Ember shouts under her breath, then pauses. "Wait, why can't I say ****?" She'll have to look for the profanity filter later. For now, footfalls stomp overhead and down the stairs.

"Who goes there? I'm armed and not afraid to break a few bones." Wixley shouts, their bedside morning star grasped tightly in hand. Their eyes search the room for potential burglars before they relax on Ember sniffling at the bar. "Oh, you're up early."

"Couldn't sleep. I'm sorry, I didn't mean to wake you." Wixley rubs the back of their neck, looking back and forth between Ember and their morning star. They tuck the weapon behind their back, awkwardly.

"No, no, you didn't wake me. I just… uh.. Wanted to get a drink… at three in the morning… With my morning star. You look like you could use one, too."

"What, a drink or a morning star?"

"A drink, you landlubber." They place their weapon on the counter with a thud of forgotten strength before searching over shelves. Their fingers skim over labels and make the bottles clink softly in the night.

"Isn't it a little too early for that?" They scoff at Ember, a bottle in their hand.

"You wound me. I didn't open this place by putting all my eggs into the 'wine and spirits' basket. I have plenty of other baskets, thank you very much! I'm sure I can fix something up that'll keep you on your feet for the rest of the day." Wixley crushes a handful of coffee beans and pours them into a mug. They pull bottles from over and under the counter, peppering, wincing, and grimacing here and there after pouring too much or spilling a little over the rim. It's touch and go at first but eventually, a drink lands in Ember's hand, and the first sip comforts her like a warm blanket on a rainy day.

"It's not bad," Ember smiles over the rim. Wixley scrunches up their face.

"Not bad? It's fantastic! You just don't want to admit I'm getting a hang of this" Ember giggles into her cup until her smile evaporates. "You surprised me, you know?"

"How so?"

"Well, from what I hear about the other new arrivals is that most people find their calling," they say, pointing at the book, "and head straight to the very gates of hell, or the bounty boards, whichever's closer. Haven't had anyone stay the night before. You have your cat friend, so what's stopping you?"

"I don't know." Ember chews thoughtfully on the cherry garnish. "Same reason you stopped the hero thing and took up bartending, I imagine." Wixley settles in, leaning against the counter.

"You can only fight oh so many sea serpents before your eyes start searching for something else, something quieter. My favorite part of adventuring was going to the tavern and asking the bartender what's going on around town. The -best- part! No two taverns were exactly alike, you know? And the names they'd give those places? A-mazing!!! Now I'm one of them, with a place that has a name, telling people what I hear around town," Wixley grinned, pleased with themself.

"You should be proud."

"I am proud." Ember takes a careful sip, tapping her fingers along her cup. She looks into the beverage.

"I don't want this to end." She said, finally. "I know it's stupid, but this is nice. Even without the magic and the quests, I like spending my time here. I want to make it last. Every step I take out that door brings me closer to the end, and I'm not ready for the credits to roll."

"Right. Credits. Rolling." Wixley nods evenly. "I'm going to pretend I know what that means. I don't know what sea serpents you've been up against, but I understand how it feels to take a minute before picking yourself up and going back to the next monster. You take your time, kid. If it means more help around the dining room then stay as long as you like. World's not burning down anytime soon now is it?" They chuckle, heartily. Then their face grows a touch more serious. "Just promise me you'll head out there when you're ready. There's a whole world outside this tavern. Be a shame if you deny it the pleasure of your company."

The doors of the Sip & Sail burst open, and a woman clad in leather stands in the entryway. Sweat trickles down her face, matting her black hair, cut short and efficiently. Time freezes and Emma is hit with a startling realization. *"Oh no, she's stunning!"* She was stunning. She pulls down her red mask, gasping for breath, "water... Please." Wixley grabs a water skin and vaults over the bar. Ember rushes to the newcomer with a chair in hand. She takes the water skin and empties it, coughing into her gloves and slumping in the chair.

"Easy there, you're going to pass out if you keep that up," Wixley warns her.

"I gotta- I gotta get out of here. Are... you players? Please tell me at least one of you is a player." Wixley looks at Ember who's still speechless from the newcomer's beauty. It takes a nudge to snap her back to reality.

"... -I am," Ember answers, "I'm Ember. Sorry."

"Percy. We can exchange handles later. Ember, can you log out?"

"I mean, I guess so, I logged out like thirty minutes ago."

"I'm not talking about thirty minutes ago, I'm talking about now. Right now. Can. You. Log. Out." Ember opens up her menu, and flips to the settings tab, staring into the horizon just as Wixley described.

"That's funny, there was a button here a few minutes ago. Maybe they're installing another patch? Do you think it got shuffled around or something?" The newcomer shakes Ember's arm so she exits her settings. When she sees her hand Ember blushes and pulls away.

"I don't think so. I can't log out either and you're the only other player I've met in this starting zone. The help desk and the forums are nowhere to be found and there's no way to access social media. The NPCs don't know anything about it, either, they just keep giving me combat hints!"

"What are you two talking about?" Wixley asked, "It's like you two are speaking an entirely different language. Did you two rehearse this? What does any of this mean?" Wixley turns to Ember who's doing everything in her power to hold back a smile.

"It means we're trapped here, Wixley."

Chapter 4: Disconnect

"I believe in destiny just enough to buy tarot cards but not enough to scare me whenever I draw the tower."
-Claire Stevenson

Claire blinks away the sleep from her eyes and the mid-morning sun keeps her from slumbering further. Her room is bathed in pink, blue, and purple hues that pierce through the crystalline shapes of a privacy screen fixed to her window. Star decals dot her walls and crystals glitter on shelves. There are no posters plastered in Claire's room. Art hangs on her walls, her art. Bold strikes, cunning flourishes. The imagery shifts and blends until you see what you want to see in her pieces.

She reaches over her nightstand for her phone, unlocking it with her yawning face to start her morning ritual. Her palate cleanser from kaleidoscopic dreams: Scrolling through news feeds and group chats, checking to see what she's missed through the night. Some would call it doom-scrolling, but Claire wears doom well: under the surface where no one can find it.

Her feed is flooded with the same story. *'Massive Multiplayer Outrage: Reality Realty offers a formal apology for the difficulties their player base is experiencing over the recent launch of their latest Virtual Reality MMORPG: Legends of Galhalla. Families all over the globe are reporting comatose players. The affected players show no response to external stimuli and a loss of overall motor functions, effectively trapping the players in-game. Reality Realty's Public Relations Officer, Blake Preston, had this to say."*

"Our programmers are working 'round the clock to find a solution to this problem. We advise against removing the headset manually at this time. A hard disconnect may lead to a series of long-term complications, including death."

"Global retail outlets are pulling their products off the shelves…'

"Damn, that's crazy," Claire says to herself. She travels down her newsfeed, but the story persists even on feeds that have no relation to the MMO. It frustrates her. Ultimately she decides it's time to stop scrolling and heads downstairs with yesterday's cereal bowl. The kitchen is quiet and devoid of life. Dad's already left for work and her brother… "must be sleeping in," she reasons as she passes his door. Claire puts the dish in the sink and begins to walk to the fridge, but she can hear her brother's words ringing in her ears.

Claire's shoulder angel gets the better of her as her hands find a sponge and a bottle of soap from under the counter. Although she loathes getting her hands wet, she cleans her bowl, one less thing for her brother to worry about. She leaves the bowl in the drying rack and opens the fridge to make today's bowl of cereal. The sugary, colorful marshmallow medley clashes almost violently with her stoic demeanor and dark rocker sleeping shirt, but Claire's loathed to part with her favorite cereal. She glides up the stairs and is about to pass her brother's room when something nags at her.

Claire stands in front of the door, trying to decide between knocking on the door and letting him sleep well into the afternoon. After the dinner they had last night, she would have wanted to sleep the day away too, if she had let her dad's words affect her as much as they affected her brother. She rolls her eyes, *"I guess I should be a good sister and check up on him."* Three knocks hit her brother's door. "Morning time, lazy butt. Wake up before you miss breakfast again." No response.

Three more knocks hit the door. Nothing. *"If I open this door and you're doing something gross in there I'm going to need so much therapy."* Claire opens the door slowly and enters the room. "Hey…" The quiet hum of his computer fills the air, its fans spin at a steady pace cooling down the heated hardware. She sees a brother-shaped lump on the bed, under the covers, wires snake their way from the console to the pillow.

"I was kidding when I called you a robot in front of my friends. The wires are a nice touch though." She walks through a floor dotted with small islands of discarded laundry until she reaches his bed. Claire grabs two fistfuls of blankets and shakes her head, bracing herself. *"I don't want to do this, I don't want to do this…"* Claire pulls the covers from the bed. "Oh, thank god you're fully clothed!" Her relief is short-lived though, once her eyes find the VR visor clamped over her brother's face. "Oh shit! How'd you even get one of these?" She digs her phone out of her pocket and starts calling their dad.

'Hello, you've reached the voicemail of Henry Stevenson, I'm unable to get to the ph-…' Claire hangs up and dials again. *'Hello, you've reached*

the voicemail of Henry Stevenson,' and she keeps reaching it, again and again only to head straight to voicemail. Each call chips away at her stony exterior until it breaks and she dials three more numbers. The operator answers.

"911 what's your emergency?"

"My name is Claire Stevenson, I live at 15 Nightingale Lane. My brother's not waking up. It's the game, the VR one."

"An ambulance is on its way, please remain calm, and don't try to move him or anything. If it helps you feel any better he's not the only one. The EMTs know what they're doing at this point-..." *-click-* Claire ends the call. She opens up her messenger and texts her dad.

"Hey, I just called 911. Pick up the phone." She crosses her arms and stares at her brother. Her vision starts to blur through her tears. The adrenaline shakes her fingers as she scrolls through her contacts for someone else to call. *'The number you have dialed is not in service...'* She ends the call, angry at herself for calling her mom's old number. This time she takes her time to make sure she's calling the right person. The line rings.

"Hello?"

"Aunt Carmen? It's... It's Claire."

"Claire? Are you ok? You sound like you're crying. What's wrong?"

"He's... He's not... Waking up! And dad's not answering! I don't know what else to do!" Claire sobs into the phone.

"Honey, honey, slow down. Did you call 911?" Claire nods. It takes a minute for her to realize that her aunt can't see that through the phone.

"Y-yes..."

"Good, I'll be right over there, ok? Just try to stay calm. I'll try to get a hold of your father." The ambulance arrives and so does Aunt Carmen, a lively woman with wild hair who always gives the best hugs. She wears her face with the sort of cheer you don in the face of danger, holding Claire's shoulders and assuring her that things will work out in the end. The paramedics set up an IV and check her brother's vitals. One of them approaches Carmen with heavy bags under her eyes. There's no telling how long she's been answering calls like this one, but by her tone alone Carmen's nephew wasn't the first.

"Are you the boy's mother?" She asks Carmen.

"I'm his aunt."

"Well, ma'am, his vitals look good. He's still in there, just sleeping, like a coma. We've been getting a lot of these. Given the circumstances, we can't take him to the hospital-"

"What do you mean you can't take him to the hospital? Can't you just unplug it?" Carmen moves over to the computer, but the paramedic intercepts her with an agility that betrays her overworked state.

"It doesn't work that way, ma'am. Trust me, you want to keep that thing on him." She points at the wires as if they were a nest of vipers. "I've seen what happens when you try to take it off. It's not pretty. We don't know how long this thing's going to last so keep him comfy. I suggest you find a good pair of adult diapers to start."

"Are you serious?"

"Deadly so. Watch out for bed sores. Get a hold of your primary to set him up with a feeding tube. Kid looks like he needs it, no offense." She looks at Carmen and her expression softens a bit. "Look, I know this is tough for y'all. But he's safe, all his limbs are there. He still has all of his organs. You just have to wait for this kind of thing to run its course." She digs into her pocket and fishes out a card. "It's not much, but the company that's responsible for this mess has a customer service number. I'd give it a minute before calling them since their phones are ringing off the hook, but It's a good place to start." The paramedics wrap up their supplies and head out the door leaving Carmen and Claire to contemplate in the front hall.

"You ok, kiddo?" Claire nods. "Good, good. This is nothing. We survived a plague for god's sake." Carmen punches the customer service number into her phone. "Why don't you check on your brother? I got a few calls to make." Claire makes it halfway up the stairs before the front door unlocks. Mr. Stevenson charges to an abrupt stop, the smell of fresh grease clings tightly to his jumpsuit.

"I saw the ambulance, is he ok?" He asks Carmen.

"He's upstairs. Henry, the paramedics said he's in a coma."

"I'm going to pay thousands of dollars because my son is taking a nap?"

"Is that really what we're focusing on right this second? Your son's not responding. If you're so concerned about money, I can lend a hand-..."

"You'd like that, wouldn't you?" Mr. Stevenson sneers.

46

"No, but Sarah would." Tension swirls in the air, thick and heavy like smog.

"It's not just about the money, Carmen. I had to leave in the middle of my shift. There's a decent chance that I won't have a job to come back to because of this. When he wakes up I'm gonna-"

"Do what Henry? Ground him? Blame him for something he couldn't have possibly seen coming? You're unbelievable!"

"I don't have time for this."

"You have all the time in the world now. Besides, you can't afford to let the lights go out. They said it could scramble his head if he gets disconnected. I'm staying here and you're going to accept it. Do you want to do something about it? Here!" Carmen presses the customer service number into Henry's chest. "Go make yourself useful."

Carmen storms up the stairs past Claire to check on her nephew. Henry stares over the card and runs his fingers over the Reality Realty logo. He looks up the stairs to see Claire sitting on the steps, looking at him with her face between the balusters.

"I'm not the bad guy here, Claire. I know it probably doesn't look that way, but I'm just trying to protect my family."

"I know dad. You just have a funny way of showing it." Henry takes in a deep breath, another log placed on the dam that's keeping the waters of a meltdown from washing over him.

"Stay here, do what your Aunt Carmen tells you to do. I'm going out. There's no way I'm going to spend my first day of unemployment on hold for hours." He hops into his truck and fires up the engine. One corporate address later and he's on the road, staring at the family photo he keeps next to the speedometer.

The streets are nearly empty as Henry's truck grumbles out of the neighborhood and towards the city. They stay empty, nearly as empty as they were during the plague. Henry's hands tighten over the steering wheel as his mind takes him back a decade. When the truck was a little quieter and he was a little leaner and Sarah was still alive.

His son was barely able to sit himself up before Henry sat him in front of a screen to watch all the greats. The Voidfarer Saga, Raiders of the Lost Spark, and Carolina Holmes were all movies that made him who he was and Henry was eager to share them with his son. Sarah had watched a few and introduced Henry to a couple classics of her own, but one way or another she would stand up halfway through the movie to adjust something or put away something else. Claire would tell him later on that Sarah might have had a little ADHD, and maybe she was right. His son had no issue staying in front of the screen, and for that Henry was proud. Until he started distancing himself from Henry, running away into a different screen in his room.

Chapter 5: Escort

"It's dangerous to go alone, so bring friends… and a designated healer… and a good sword… supplies… maybe a wagon."
 -Mx. Wixley, Hero of Harbortown

Dawn breaks over Harbortown with a yoke-colored sun that bathes the fluttering sails in golden hues. It spills through the stained-glass windows of the Sip & Sail bringing form to the dust motes floating around the dining room. Wixley looks at Ember and Percy as if they've lost their heads. "What do you mean you're trapped? You two can leave anytime you want! There's the door right in front of you, it's not even locked!" Ember shakes her head.

"It's not like that, Wixley. Do you think maybe you can make another one of those drinks you made me? Percy looks like she could use one." Wixley nods, standing up from one knee to walk over to the bar.

"NPC's." Percy spits the word out of the corner of her mouth and shoots a glance at Ember. "I don't need a drink. I need to get out of here." She eyes Ember closely. "Why aren't you concerned? You can't go home, either. You know that, right?" Ember jumps up and stammers quickly.

"I know! I just feel like you're freaking out enough for both of us. No offense, but I don't see how adding to it will fix anything." This was rich coming from Emma, who was voted 'Most Likely to

49

have a panic attack,' last year. On any other day of the week, Emma would be right there with Percy, passing the proverbial paper bag to hyperventilate into. Not today though. Today is the best day of the rest of Ember's life! Except if she shows any hint of it Percy's going to think she's insane.

"Why is your face all scrunched up like that?" Percy asks.

"What? Oh, I- ... Don't worry about it." Ember cursed the game for reading her expressions so precisely. "I don't suppose there's another player around here that can help you- I mean, us out?" Percy shakes her head.

"Not in Harbortown. I've checked. I think everyone else has already grouped up so they could power-level through the forest. There's a big quest hub called Hammerfall on the other side of it. But the forest is crawling with high-level mobs and my sneaking can only get me so far."

"Hmmm, well, looks like the world's on fire." Percy tilts her head and purses her lips together. "It's nothing. I'll help you get through the forest. I'm sure we'll find someone in Hammerfall that can help us. Let me get dressed and grab my cat." Ember runs upstairs to put on her best and only pair of wizard's robes from her inventory, even though she could have switched her apparel downstairs, the thought of changing in front of Percy made her uneasy.

"I was comfy!" Chance's protest devolves into a series of chirping meows from the bed. Eventually, she gives in to Ember's prodding and grudgingly takes her place on Ember's shoulders. Together they head back downstairs.

"I'll see you later, Wixley. World's on fire." Wixley's eyes beam with excitement. They shake their fists and their muscles tense as a smile grows wide on their face.

"Yes, Ember!" They cheer. "Go forth! Carve your legend into the thick, scaly hide of destiny!" Ember smiles back at the bartender.

"Take care of Ratlantis for me while I'm gone," she calls out from over her shoulder, pointing at the treaty on the wall with an apologetic smile. Wixley slumps over the bar.

"No, Ember! Stay here and carry on your diplomatic duties," Their mock cries carry out of the windows and into Drain Street.

"You're a good friend. Keep an eye on the post, I'll send you some letters," Ember says over her shoulder. "Alright Perc', lead the way."

"It's Percy." She briskly walks past Ember and out through the open door.

"Right, Percy." Together they meander their way side-by-side with fishmongers and cheese wheelers until they reach the outskirts of Harbortown. The sand and rock give way to tufts of grass, sparse at first until they reach a thick blanket of crisp green blades growing wild and long. Percy watches Ember closely, whenever Ember looks back at her Percy looks the other way, trying to find interest in the plain shrubbery around them. Eventually, the silence is too much for Percy.

"So, what's it like for you? You know, back home."

"Oh, it's alright. I mean it's real life, you know? I play games, I go to school."

"Do you have a family?"

"I do, my dad and my sister, Claire."

"Y'all close?"

"I am with my sister. But my dad and I don't see eye-to-eye as much as I would like."

"Why's that?" Ember exhales.

"It's a long story." Percy looks ahead of them and back to Ember.

"It's a long road." Ember sighs. "And I'm bored."

"He has a certain way things need to get done. If you don't do it his way then you're wrong and how dare you suggest anything in the first place. It'd be fine if I just caved in and gave him what he wanted, but I don't think I can do that anymore."

"It's not fine," Percy said matter-of-factly. So much so that it startled Ember.

"What?"

"It's not fine. You are your own person. Some people go their whole lives without figuring that out. Have you ever tried telling him that?"

"No, not yet. We fight over everything, I'm kind of done fighting."

"Well, maybe you should tell him. You're not going to get anywhere if you keep your head down." Ember nods to that.

"Thanks, I'll keep that in mind." The gentle rhythm of rough talons crunching gravel can be heard from behind, accompanied by the harsh, wooden creaking of wagon wheels desperate for oil. A portly elf sits in the box seat of a bird-drawn cart, smoking through a long, curved pipe. His cheeks are full and cheerful, his clothes just a few notches above modest, the telltale signs of a humble shopkeeper. He rides beside them and doffs his hat, bowing his head as the cart stops. An exclamation mark hovers above him.

"Why hello there young travelers! Don't suppose you're heading through Tanglewood Forest, are you?"

"Not interested. Buzz off, bird man." Percy spits. Ember leans into her in a hushed panic of sorts.

"Woah, Woah, there's no need to pick the mean dialogue options right off the bat, we barely know this guy."

"Precisely, we don't know him. He could be bad news and I'm not wasting any niceties if he ends up being a ****."

"At least let me talk to him. I wanna see what he's all about." Percy scowls and crosses her arms.

"Fine, go ahead. Enjoy the 'roleplay.'" Ember turns to address the elf.

"Sorry, my friend and I are in a bit of trouble. I'm Ember and this is Percy, we're trying to reach Hammerfall."

"Hammerfall? Well lucky me. Clover and I were just on our way there." He pats the battle chicken, tenderly. "Sylas Dewdrop's the name, but my friends call me Dewy. No one answered my bounty board request back in town, so might as well try going about the journey alone. But, I'd feel a lot safer if you two would accompany me. I still have the coin if you're willing and I'll let you feed Clover!" The battle chicken clucks at the mention of food. Percy takes Ember aside.

"It's an escort quest. We don't have time for quests."

"It's a free ride that we'll get paid for taking. Besides, we need the experience and I don't want to say no and end up following him anyway. That'd be so awkward!" Percy stares at Ember as if she just turned green.

"... Who thinks about that stuff?"

"I'm with her," the cart driver chimes in. "I don't want to absentmindedly follow you two either, it feels a little creepy." Percy throws her hands up in the air.

"Ugh! Fine! We'll take your quest. This better not be one of those long-winded cutscenes or I'll make you a cut scene, got it?" Percy flashes her daggers at Sylas and Ember lowers them just as quickly.

"Alright, easy killer. After you." They hop up into the back of the cart. With a fine whistle, Dewy prompts Clover to tow the cart through the woods. Sunlight pierces through the openings in the canopy leaving dappled pools on the forest floor. The pools shrink into ponds and then into puddles as they move deeper into the forest until the cart is enveloped in a desert of darkness underneath the heavy canopy.

Sylas shakes one of the hanging canisters on his belt. The liquid inside glows bright orange and yellow, bright enough to stand in for a torch, casting shadows on the forest floor. All the while the wheels creak along the dirt road. Ember looks at Percy and then the cart driver.

"So… Dewdrop, what do you do for a living?"

"What? Sorry, you don't realize just how loud your cart is until you have passengers." He chuckles mostly to himself.

"We're making far too much noise." Percy warns Ember over the sound of the wheels, "We should stop the cart."

"I don't see how we can shop for art around here," Dewy told Percy. "It's all leaves and twigs! The closest painter's back in Old Harbortown." He said, gesturing behind them. "Nope, not a lot of art shops here in the Tanglewood."

"That's not what I said." Percy groans. "Ugh, do something, Ember!"

"Hang on, I think I got it." Ember flips through the pages until she finds one of the spells she dismissed earlier in the cellar. She recites a few choice words. Chance's eyes flash a green light and a thick slimy substance pours from Ember's palm. "Gah! This is so much worse than how it's described in the book," she scowls in disgust. Percy stares at her hands.

"Ember, your hand is… leaking."

"I know, it's a spell called 'Grease.' Maybe we could use it to make the wheels quieter."

"That's… not bad, actually." For the first time since they met Percy gave her a half-smile. She wipes it off her face as soon as it arrives. "Well, don't let me distract you. You're getting it everywhere and I don't like slime. Even if this isn't technically real." Ember drips the grease onto the wheels and in moments the only sound in the forest is Clover's talon beats. Sylas lets out a low whistle.

"Now that is worlds better." Sylas nods in approval. "I'm ashamed I didn't think to grease the wheels before leaving. The conversations I could have had in this cart! The details I've missed!... Wait! Was that stout-kin woman hitting on me?

Gods, that was ten years ago. Oh well, you were saying?" Ember furrows her brow but decides to leave it well enough alone.

"Right, so what do you do? Is cart transport your passion?"

"What? No, I'm a chemist. I own Dewdrop's Droppers and Stoppers down on Briney Boulevard. I'm hoping to expand into Hammerfall, the whole place is pretty much set up, but my last shipment ran astray in these accursed woods. I'm taking life by the reins, so to speak."

"Wait, what happened to the last person?" Ember said before getting a tap on her shoulder.

"High-level-mobs," Percy coughs into her glove.

"Could have been bandits or wolves." Sylas shrugs. "The Harbortown loggers like to spin tales about how dangerous the forest can be, but I think they're just trying to get out of a hard day's work. Now my last man? Can't say for certain. Maybe he fled with the cargo. Though I doubt he'd get much gold selling fertilizer! Well, magically-infused fertilizer but fertilizer nonetheless." Dewdrop slaps his knee at the thought.

The cart leans abruptly to one side before slamming back onto the ground, sending Clover into a screeching panic. "Woah, girl, woah! Ahh hells, I think I ran something over." They stop and hop off, huddling around the misshapen earth. "Hmmm, looks like a root." He stares up at the tree it belongs to.

"Aww, it's shaped like a rabbit," Ember said. The resemblance is uncanny, almost as if another traveler whittled into the root to pass the time. But then the root twitches.

"I don't think it just -looks- like a rabbit, Ember." Percy's fears are warranted. Chance hisses as the rabbit has the fight drained out of it by the twisted root. The root's petrifying grasp clings tightly to its prize as bark wraps around its prey, hungrily. The bark-encased rabbit stops moving.

"What the ****?!?!" Ember screams.

"Everybody back in the cart!" Sylas orders as they pile on into the cart.

"Drive, Dewdrop! Drive!" Percy screams, patting his shoulder. His sharp whistle sends Clover thundering through the forest, sending wayward feathers down the road. As they fall to the ground hungry vines shoot forth to snatch the feathers only to shake in disappointment once they realize there's nothing fleshy to claim.

"Am I seeing things or are the branches coming in closer?" Ember peers behind them. They were closing in... searching for the cart with insatiable zeal.

"So that's why they call it 'Tanglewood'," Sylas wipes the sweat from his brow.

"Perc, did you know about the evil plants? Because it would've been nice to know about the evil plants." Ember flings bolts of fire at tireless twigs.

"The hell I did." She said, slashing at the encroaching branches, "This is new. I went back to town before getting this far. I figured we'd be up against bears. Or bandits. Or bear-riding bandits." They whizz past a tangle of vines that constrict around an abandoned cart like a forestry fist. Ember blinks at the other driver, entombed in the bark.

"Umm Dewy, I think I know what happened to the last guy."

The crash happens in seconds. Faster than they can think. Clover trips over a root system. The cart tumbles overhead and into the underbrush. The world turns upside down then right side up. Then impact. The wind is knocked out of Ember. She reaches for her Tome, coughing into choking vines, but passes out. Her fingers barely make contact. Slashing knives and a hissing familiar are the last things she hears before her vision fades.

Chapter 6: Freemium

"Grandpa always said 'there's no such thing as a free lunch,' and it's true. I've never gotten something for free without having to pay for it later."
-Henry Stevenson

"... -pulled off all related products in response to the recent recall.." Henry switches the station, *"... -a virtual catastrophe well underway and Calvin Sinclair remains tight-lipped regarding the investigation into his company's massive VR failure."* Henry changes the station again until he hears something he can drum his fingers to.

His truck comes to a halt at the corporate offices of Reality Realty: a cold, mirrored tower that looms over a web of roadways circulating through downtown Del Aire. To his dismay he's not alone. Hundreds of angry protesters mob the entrance to the lobby in a scene described in real-time by nearby reporters and vloggers. They bang at the windows and shake their fists, most of them are carrying signs. Henry tries to make his way through the crowd, but they are many and they are volatile.

"Please, return to your homes. The situation is being handled." A security guard speaks through a loudspeaker. The crowd shakes in anger and their yells swell through the surrounding streets. "This is a corporate office building, people work here."

"Give us back our children!" A woman cries.

"We're doing everything we can."

"Tell that to my husband!" Yells a man from the crowd.

"Please, I just want my son back," Henry shouts.

"If you don't clear the premises willingly we will be obligated to use force." Police car sirens stop their call as their passengers pour into the streets, bottling the mob up. Henry notices a protester next to him with shiny, black boots, digging into his bag. He stuffs a long piece of cloth into a bottle of alcohol.

"Hey buddy, I don't think that's a good idea." The man ignores Henry as he lights the cloth. "Buddy. Hey, stop that!" Henry grabs the man's shirt and balls it in his fist, loosening the buttons to reveal a badge. "Aren't you supposed to be protecting and serving?" The man wrestles out of Henry's grasp and throws his destructive spirit. Henry attempts to intercept the bottle, but his fingers are inches away, grazing it. The flaming bottle arcs through the air and smashes against the ground near the guards, spreading fire in its wake. The policemen ready their batons and go to town, arresting anyone close enough to put in handcuffs.

Henry punches the firestarter and knocks him out cold, he drops to the ground as the crowd scatters. Henry swims through the chaos and ducks into an alleyway. "I'm not getting my truck anytime soon," he says to himself as he watches the cops corral the remaining protesters. His fist throbs in his other hand, "can't believe I just punched a cop." The mirrored tower stares back at Henry. A voice from behind startles him.

"You picked a hell of a place to take your break, pal. We just had a riot in front of the lobby. You must be the new trainee." A person in a nearly identical jumpsuit addresses Henry. They're younger than Henry, by far, with a mop of hair dyed green.

"Oh, I'm sorry I don't..." Henry pivots, "...know what I was doing, just needed some fresh air."

"I feel yah, the warehouse can get a little stuffy. The foreman's gonna blow a fuse if we keep this up though, we should head back." They lead him out of the alley after giving Henry a cursory once-over. "Damn, where's your name tag, dude?"

"Uh, I didn't get one."

"What am I going to do with you, guy?"

"Henry."

"Nice to meet you, Henry. Call me Sage." Henry and his new trainer make their way through security and into the large roll-up doors of the warehouse. Thousands of boxes march from their respective eighteen-wheelers and retreat back into a maze of conveyor belts. "Man, this recall is going to suck."

"Where are they all going?"

"We're sending them back to the eggheads in research and development. But if you ask me I think this problem's a lot bigger than a few busted headsets," they shrug, "Not my monkey, not my circus, you know?"

"Yeah," Henry agrees, "but say this was your monkey, how'd you go about fixing it?"

"All this external stuff we're doing's just to stop us from getting sued by -more- people. This feels like a software thing rather than a hardware thing. The product works, it just works -too- well. If I was in charge I'd search through the game's code with a fine-tooth comb. You got to get in there to fix it because there's no way in hell we'd be able to get to each headset to troubleshoot it."

Sage leads Henry to the back of the warehouse and into a training room. The room sports two chairs, a table, a TV, and a plethora of posters devoted to safe practices and procedures as well as the ever-present dangers of corporate espionage. "So don't hate me, but we have some training videos to get through, well I don't, but you do. But if you ace your quiz fast enough we'll see about getting you forklift-certified. That's where it's at. I'm going to see about getting you a new name tag. You don't need adult supervision, right?"

"I have kids your age. I'm sure I'll be fine."

"Cool, I'll be back." Sage presses play, leaving Henry alone in the room with Calvin Sinclair on the screen in a sharp suit. He's handsome and pale with hands that have never known a hard day's work and a smile untarnished by most of life's ills.

"...When I assumed my parent's real estate company I was in my twenties. But I couldn't keep my eyes from wandering. There are limits to physical space, limits I was never comfortable with accepting. We went to the moon because we grew tired of what this world had to offer. I had to find the next moon. When I told my parents about my plans to expand our business into what I call 'Virtual Realty' they were less than thrilled. But, I was telling them, you see? I didn't ask them. You don't ask permission to make history…"

"I've had enough of this guy." Henry cracks the door open and sneaks out of the training room. He walks back into the loud din of the warehouse. A single number among hundreds of workers engaged in a barely stable ballet. It's a dizzying display, but not too far off from his own workplace, save for one addition he bumps into, the foreman, a monitor affixed to a mobile platform with its scanners fixed on Henry.

"Please report back to your workstation." It commands Henry.

"Uhh, I was on my way to the restroom."

"Insert ID badge to clock out for Bio-Break."

"Shit," Henry thinks. "… I lost it."

"Scanning facial features. Facial features: not recognized. Employee ID: not found. Alerting Security." Henry sidesteps the robot, power-walks to the nearest fire alarm, and pulls down the handle. The warehouse workers shuffle to the emergency exit, and Henry tries to blend in as much as possible. The crowd heads out the doors, abuzz with more energy than a triple-shot. Henry breathes a sigh of relief, he looks like he's in the clear.

It becomes less clear once everyone settles into their designated muster stations. Security guards wade through the workers, scanning IDs with their work phones. Henry inches further away until he corners himself in the yard, his back to a chain link fence. One of the guards looks at their phone, then back at Henry.

"Hey, you!" Henry takes his cue to scale the fence. He hoists his massive frame until his fingers hit the barbed wire. Henry hits the ground flat after a hand takes hold of his ankle and yanks him down. Two guards hoist him up to his feet, but Henry struggles in their grasp. Henry manages to land a punch and the workers go wild, cheering and recording the ordeal on their devices. They crowd around them, an impenetrable wall of bodies separating Henry from escape.

He puts up his fists and musters what he can from his boxing days. A left hook, block, duck into a haymaker. One guard drops to the ground. The other lunges toward Henry, grabbing his waist and charging him into the chain link fence. Henry bounces from the links and raises his bloody fists before slamming them into his attacker's back. The security guard crumbles to the ground as the crowd roars around Henry.

A giant walks through the crowd and sets his sight on Henry. His neck cracks around thick cords of muscle. The workers clear around him like a school of fish around a hungry shark. He breaks free from the crowd and cracks his knuckles as he enters the informal arena. Henry steps over the second guard after spitting out a tooth. He wipes the blood from his mouth. Once he sees his new challenger his jaw drops to the floor.

"You gotta be kidding me," Henry wheezes, "alright, big guy, come at me. I could do this all day." The giant guard reaches for his belt, unclips a remote that's dwarfed by his massive hands, and points it at Henry. With the press of a button, twin electrodes fire into Henry sending him convulsing to the floor. "Ch-ch-ch-cheater!" Henry passes out to a chorus of pained groans.

When Henry wakes up, he's in a room with no windows and no doors. White walls blend seamlessly with the floor and ceiling. If his feet weren't physically touching the ground he wouldn't believe it was even there. He lifts his hands only to realize they're restrained to the chair he's sitting on.

"Oh good, you're awake." A smooth, familiar voice filters into the room in condescending waves.

"Who's there?" Henry asks the open air.

"Physically? Just you, my friend. I saw how well-versed you are with your fists. I'd rather you not unleash your fury for the time being." Wall tiles separate into millions of hexagons that pull together into the mosaic image of Mr. Sinclair. "Mr. Stevenson, is it?" His image is holding Henry's license.

"That's correct."

"I'm sure I need no introduction. You saw our training video, after all. Did you enjoy your free tour of our facilities? I'm sure you found the security personnel helpful, yes?"

"As helpful as a Gregslist dentist. Tell me why I shouldn't sue you for all you've got."

"-Tut- -tut- Mr. Stevenson. It's all about having the right perspective. Some might see your actions today and use phrases like 'corporate espionage' and 'assault.' I could ruin you, you know? Send you off to the authorities." Henry fumes. "But I won't do that. We're going to handle this all in-house. Civil."

"What's that supposed to mean? You're going to let me go?" Calvin shakes his head.

"Yes… and no. I'll give you the means to find your son if you handle a personal matter of mine. Do a good enough job and I'll make sure this whole issue is placed solidly behind us."

"What do you want?"

"A great many things, Mr. Stevenson. But I need you to deliver a package, somewhere I can't go."

"Don't you have a whole fleet of drivers? You're a resourceful guy, aren't you?"

"Resourceful, yes. Cunning, handsome, this is also true. But none of that will help me here. But you? Someone with drive? Ambition? I'm sure you're more than capable."

"Listen, even if I was gonna take you up on your offer, I'm gonna need something a bit more substantial than that. How do I know you're not going to screw me over?"

"Ahh, that's the trick, isn't it? I'll let you in on a little secret, Mr. Stevenson: you don't. Either you do my bidding or you can enjoy a leisurely stay at the Del Aire Penitentiary. Now, while you mull over the illusion of choice, I have a plane to catch. Safe travels, Mr. Stevenson, and mind the updates!" Calvin Sinclair's smile is the last thing Henry sees as a headset visor clamps down over his eyes.

"No wait, don't!" The visor powers on and Henry's body goes limp.

Chapter 7: Party

"Hint: when casting a spell be mindful of the spell's target area. You never want to harm your fellow party members. Or yourself!"
-RR

Ember can't tell what woke her up first: her throbbing headache or the slow, dripping drops hitting her forehead from up in the stalactites. Her vision comes to her in bits and pieces, nearby morels light the darkness up in orange and yellow bioluminescent spores. She quiets her breathing as the sound of damp footsteps plopping over stone grows closer. The creature is humanoid-shaped, roughly her height. Twisting bark makes up most of its skin with an ax head buried deep where its clavicle would be. Its composite eyes are made from the same glowing morels lighting the room.

'****. This.****.' Ember thinks to herself. It creaks towards a bundle of vines wrapped around a giant root spilling from the cave wall. The creature places a tendriled hand on the vine bundle, its eyes glow brighter as the bundle shudders and grunts in pain. It shakes its head, grabbing a handful of green, clumpy soil from a nearby bag, the same bag Ember sat on in Dewy's cart. It sprinkles the contents at the base of the root and turns to another root pillar and its eyes glow. This time the bundle stirs until a twiggy arm bursts forth from the cocoon. Another tree monster emerges from the plant matter, leaving behind a pile of discarded clothes. The two creatures stare at Ember, then stomp out of the cave.

As soon as they depart Ember wiggles frantically, trying to get out of her constraints, but the roots don't yield. "Chance!" She half-whispered and half-shouted. "You out there? Percy? Dewy?" Ember whimpers. "I don't wanna be a plant thing!!!"

"Your friends aren't here." The other mass of vines wheezed. "... But I can take you to them."

"Gah! Talking vines!"

"Not yet, I'm not." Ember stares warily at the coughing bundle.

"Are you ok?"

"Never better, actually that's a lie. I've been better. This situation has so *mushroom* for improvement." Ember stifles a giggle.

"Oh, you have jokes? Who are you?"

"You can call me Cole."

"I'm Ember."

"We don't have a lot of time, Ember. Can you get us out of these vines? I'd do it myself, but-" Cole coughs, "I'm not exactly at my best." Ember's eyes search the inside of the cavern. Her Tome is several feet away from them, accompanied by a sword and a few gemstones. The small hoard sits on top of a stone altar carved into the rock wall. Suddenly, her pocket stirs. It terrifies Ember at first until a tiny, familiar head pops out.

"Bramble? What are you doing here?!?"

"Who are you talking to?" Cole asks. Bramble squeaks triumphantly.

"Bramble, Bramble!"

"Saying it more doesn't help me comprehend it any better."

"He's a friend!" The rat warrior produces a variety of squeaks, no doubt recounting his various, pocket-related exploits. "Bramble, I can't understand you. I need to get out of these vines, but I need my Tome to cast anything. My Tome, over there." Ember points her head toward the stone altar. Bramble spies his quarry, he controls his descent by bouncing off the vines wrapping Ember then sprints along the cavern floor before scaling the rocky cliffs. The Tome is heavy, but he manages to send it plunging toward the ground. "That's it, Bramble! You are the coolest, tiny hero!!!"

Bramble squeaks in what Ember could only imagine as a flurry of mousy curses based on the rat's rapid, heated gestures. He pushes the Tome towards her, straining against the friction. "Come on, come on!" Ember stretches as far as she can until her boot touches the paper. With her connection to the arcane re-established, Chance phases in through a wall, taking a casual look at their surroundings.

"I leave for just a moment and here you are all tied up. Not a good look for you, darling."

"Chance now is -not- the time for small talk! No, wait... maybe it is." She points a free finger at Bramble and casts the spell, shrinking enough so she could wiggle through her gnarled roots.

"-And if you call me tiny one more time! I-..." Bramble's rant is cut short with a swift

hug from a rat-sized Ember.

"I am so sorry. Thanks for helping us out. What were you doing in my pocket?" Bramble gathers himself, readjusting his leafy leathers.

"I was mapping out what lies beyond Ratlantis when I grew tired and fell asleep in a cave. The next thing I knew my refuge turns on its side and I'm off, hoisted away on a giant-riding adventure. This pocket of yours makes for a great watchtower."

"Are you going to be alright being this far away from Ratlantis?"

"Please, I live for adventure! My map of the giant lands will be the largest my kin has ever seen. With you as my underling, Ratlantis will hail me as a hero. Maybe I will tame your cat one day, and ride it into battle!"

"Alright then, back in your watchtower, you go." Ember casts Small Talk again but points the spell at Cole to regain her height. She pockets Bramble, grabs the sword from the altar, and starts chopping away, freeing her new confined confidant. Cole stiffly walks out of the cocoon, an outstretched metal gauntlet asking for their sword to which Ember obliges.

"Not bad, ever think about taking up the blade?"

"Not a chance," she laughs a little too loud, clearing her throat, "I mean, I don't see myself getting up close and personal. I'd rather not, y'know, get up close and personal. With monsters... and other people." Ember finds herself suddenly flustered.

"You have more fight in you than you'd care to admit. You and your many animal companions." Chance rubs against Cole until Ember picks her up.

"Yeah, I'm a regular princess." The paladin looks past the cave entrance.

"Your friends should be down by the clearing, I'll take you there." Together they leave the cave with

70

Ember following Cole's lead. "They dragged me off into the cave once they found out I could heal. I take it you use magic, too?" Ember nods. "They've been draining my mana. They need us to make more of them." Cole slashes at a few branches along the way as if each swing were an act of petty revenge.

"I take it they're not using Dewy's fertilizer for dirt cup desserts," Ember said.

"You'd be right. I'm sure they enjoy whatever Sylas's been cooking. You answered his bounty board, right? But then your wagon got derailed by a bunch of freaky, evil vines, yes?"

"Kinda, we found him on our way to Hammerfall. He offered us a ride."

"He left his shop? That's brave." Cole stops abruptly on the peak of a shallow hill. A fallen log separated them from the clearing. Three tree creatures stalk the area, occasionally checking on two bundles of vines grafted onto trunks.

"There's Percy and Dewy!" Ember whispered/shouted, "How are we going to get-" Before Ember could even finish what she was about to say Cole rushes in, vaulting over a log, sword in hand. "Cole? Cole!!!"

"No use in sneaking, princess!" Cole shouts behind them, "I'm a walking pile of plate!" Ember hops over the log. What starts as an anxious charge morphs into a haphazard slide on slick, dead leaves down the hill. By the time she reaches the clearing, Cole is already engaged in a battle against branches, two against one.

Ember opens her tome and casts Dice Shard. The spell manifests into three dice that roll from her fingertips until they land on their numbers. The dice then sharpen, springing from the ground and embedding themselves into plant matter. One of the creatures crumbles back into the soil and experience points flood into Ember's HUD. Its remaining companion roars at Cole, charging at them with thrashing limbs. Cole deflects what blows they can with their sword, "I got this covered! Go save your friends, princess!" Ember runs to a Percy-shaped bundle, trying to unwrap the vines.

"Percy! Are you alright?"

"Never better, well besides the whole turning-into-a-tree thing."

"I'm getting you out of here."

"No pressure, I'm rooting for you."

"Was that a pun?"

"Nope, just poor word choice." A rough and rigid hand grabs onto Ember's shoulder. Its grip is firm and menacing.

'****,' she curses to herself. The creature opens its mouth, roaring spores into the air. It lifts Ember and tosses her aside so it can work its magic on Percy. *'Think, think, think! Percy's never gonna let it go if she turns into a mushroom munchie.'* Ember had a thought. A risky and almost downright stupid thought. But if she wants to save Percy, and save her quickly, she'd have to do something that's frowned upon in most Labyrinths and Lava-Bears circles.

"What are you doing? Ember stop!" Chance demands as Ember's magic swirls on her fingertips. "That spell's radius is too wide. We're too close." Ember aims the spell just short of Percy and then braces herself. The fireball screams out of her hand, finding its mark and setting the creature on fire. It screeches, charred but still moving, trying to wave away the flames. Ember collapses, singed and aching. The creature approaches her, its mycelium maw is twisted into a fit of fungal fangs. It raises its limbs into the sky, readying for the killing blow.

Ember closes her eyes, mentally preparing for whatever this game had in store for death. But death doesn't come. She hears a flurry of knives piercing through tree bark and a sudden, heavy thud. Ember opens her eyes and Percy is standing over the tree corpse, blades slick with sticky sap.

"Hey, you finally got to stab something," Ember laughs weakly.

"Shut up," Percy said, softer than her usual cadence. Her eyes glance over Ember's burns. Percy picks her up off the ground just as Cole lands the final blow upon the last tree monster, bisecting the creature.

"That's for stealing my mana, I could have used that for spells, you thieving birch!" They stomp on the creature, ignoring the loot it's just dropped before making their way towards Ember and Percy, exhaling. "Well, I don't know about you two, but I feel much better."

"Who's the suit?" Percy asked.

"Percy, this is Cole. I found them in the same cave the mushroom men kept me."

"Charmed." They bowed, armor plates clinking with their movements.

"Right," Percy said, unimpressed. "Are you a player?"

"Aren't we all?" Cole answered, "all the world's a stage, am I right?"

"That's not what I meant. Can you log out?"

"I've been at the mercy of plant folk for days, please don't speak of logs." Percy's eyes narrow and Cole's helmet tilts to the side.

"Let's get moving before more of those things show up."

"Aren't you forgetting something?" Cole said, pointing to Dewy. Percy gives Cole a firm glance and clicks her tongue. Quick knives and quicker hands dance around Dewy, cutting just the right vines to set him free. She scoffs at Cole before helping Ember back to the road. The vines drop to the ground moments after, freeing a bewildered Dewy.

"Come on Em, let's get back to the cart." They hobble through the underbrush until they find the road and their crash site. Clover was not too far off, pecking at the dirt. Percy digs around the driver's console until she produces a stash of Dewy's health serums and starts tending to Ember's wounds.

"I don't need those, I'm fine! I'll be good after a short rest." But Percy doesn't listen, pushing the potion to Ember's lips.

"He owes you and you need it. Drink." Percy looks to the side and coughs awkwardly. "So, I'm going to need you to not do that again."

"Do what?"

"Hurt yourself. I didn't like it."

"Aww, are you going soft on me?"

"Shut up! Forget I said anything." Dewy and Cole arrive shortly after. Dewy sets to the task of repairing the cart and with Cole's help, they're able to get the cart back into working shape. "It's been real, tin man, but we gotta get moving. Have fun doing whatever it is you're doing out here," said Percy. Cole's helmet tilts in confusion,

"I was hoping to get a ride to Hammerfall. If that's alright."

"That's not a bad idea. I wouldn't mind the extra security," said Dewy.

"We could use the help, Perc. We wouldn't be standing here if it weren't for Cole." Percy looks long and hard at Ember before finally caving in.

"Fine, fine. But only because you almost died. We're not picking up any more stragglers. This little detour set us back." She turns her attention to Cole. "You can sit up there with Dewdrop," she points at the driver's seat. Cole takes their place next to the driver and with that, the party continues on the road to Hammerfall. Ember rests her head on one of the remaining sacks of fertilizer, trying to make herself as comfortable as possible in the uncomfortable silence. *'Well, at least we have a party now.'*

Chapter 8: Pirated

"Hint: everyone serves an important role on a ship, from the captain down to the cabin boy. No matter their role they are worthy of respect."
-RR

"Hello? Hello!?!?" Henry screams into thin air. His stomach turns inside out as he floats in a blue sky with fluffy white clouds. A storied landscape appears below him. "AAAAHHHHHHHHHHHH!" He screams, jamming his eyes shut. "Don't look down, don't look down, don't look down! Oh great! I'm dead aren't I?" He mumbles to himself. A wizened voice addresses him.

"Welcome, hero… To Legends of Galhalla!"

"Hello?!? There must be some kind of mistake. I shouldn't be here. Somebody get me down from here!!!" He opens his eyes and the title screen appears before Henry, three swords -*schwing*- underneath the title. "Ahhh! What is this? Those things could have killed me! I'm going to sue so hard! How do I get down from here? How do I get this thing off of me? Which one of these takes me out of here?" He picks up a sword without realizing he's picked the option on the sword's fuller. His vision pales and a moss-covered archway appears before him. Mercury pours from the other side until Henry can see himself.

"Now, who are you?"

"I'm Henry. Hello? Who are you?!? Show yourself, you Dimbledare-sounding old fart!" His words are left unanswered, leaving him alone with his reflection. He taps at the mirrored image more out of frustration than proceeding in earnest and it vanishes giving way to a captain's cabin filled with treasure. "What the hell is this?" He taps the image again and a text box appears before him. "Name... Uh... Henry." A message pops up telling him the name's already been taken. "What do you mean 'choose a new name,' it's my name!?! This is ridiculous."

Henry blusters in frustration. "Henry... Stevenson. There." The text box accepts the name and urges him to step through the archway. "Nuts to that! Is there someone I can talk to?" He turns his head and another archway appears next to the one he was looking through. Henry turns around and starts running only for another archway to form in front of him. Another turn is met with another archway, then another turn then another archway until he's surrounded by them. They circle him, drawing closer. His ears are filled with the sound of stone scraping stone. He curls in on himself, shielding his head, screaming. And then the sound stops.

Henry opens his eyes and sees wooden floorboards underneath his feet. He's on board the cabin he witnessed mere moments ago. The creaking of the chandelier overhead sounds off as the ship sways gently back and forth. He lowers his hands from over his head. His ears fill with the sound of crinkling leather sleeves belonging to a jacket he doesn't remember putting on. A pair of goggles is clenched tightly in one hand. Henry drops them onto the floor as he stands up, "Where the hell am I?"

The door opens bringing in the salty air of the outside world. Blocking the exit is the shadow of a massive construct. The automaton ducks under the head of the door and stomps threateningly toward Henry. "Get back." Henry's voice carries as much authority as a mewling kitten as he steps backward, bumping into a nearby table. His hand catches on a handle, and swings out an ornate sword from the treasure trove, aiming it at the creature. "Get Back! I'm not afraid to use this!" Its pace does not lessen as the blade scratches the heavy metal breastplate.

Henry slashes the sword, it pings off of the armor and scatters on the floor. The golem bends over to pick up the sword, but Henry leaps over its back wrapping his arms around its neck. He clings on in an attempt to choke the creature, squeezing metal plates and wooden ligaments but the golem simply stands back up lifting Henry off the floor. The metal helmet turns around to face Henry and it scares him enough that he loses his grip and lands on the floor. The automaton leans over and offers Henry a metal gauntlet.

"Captain, are you unwell? I heard screaming." A feminine voice echoes from inside the helmet. She massages her neck, settling her recently ruffled armor plates. "Apologies for startling you. I think I had a cog stuck in my throat."

"Captain?"

"HenryStevenson, Captain of *The Dreadnought*. This is you, yes?"

"Well, some of it is." The golem tilts her head.

"Captain, if you are suffering from some sort of amnesia I suggest we keep that to ourselves. The crew might mutiny." Henry stares in disbelief and stands up, taking great care in avoiding the hand stretched out before him. The golem straightens her posture and returns her hand to her side.

"What the hell are you?"

"I am P.A.C. Your Personal Adventuring Companion. Firstmate of *The Dreadnought*." P.A.C. salutes Henry who looks her up and down.

"As far as hallucinations go you're by far the weirdest. Why couldn't you be my uncle john or something more normal?"

"I am no hallucination. I am very real. Corporeal, some might say." Henry sidesteps around her and heads toward the door. "See, why would you step -around- a hallucination if I were not taking up space? You could have just walked through me if I wasn't here…"

"It's still talking," Henry says to himself.

"My pronouns are she/her, Captain," P.A.C. says sternly.

"Oh yeah? Well, mine are 'over/this,' see you in therapy, robot." Henry says over his shoulder as he opens the door and steps on the deck. Blue skies stretched all around him dotted with clouds and bright yellow sun. The salt air hits him. "Wow, this all feels so real." He looks over the taffrail and sees the ocean several stories below the ship. "AAAAAAAHHHHHH!"

The crew stops their tasks and stares at their captain stumbling backward, landing butt-first on the deck and scooting closer to the mast. "What the

**** are we doing up here?!! Somebody lower this ******* thing!!!"

"You heard the captain, prepare for landing." The helmsman pulls a lever and the airship begins its descent toward the ocean.

"Belay that, helmsman," P.A.C. orders from the door of the captain's quarters. "Maintain a steady altitude from here on out." She walks over to Henry, "a moment of your time, Captain."

"What are we doing up here? And why can't I ******* curse?"

"Now. Captain." Steam hisses above P.A.C.'s gorget as she pulls Henry up by his collar picking him up with the ease of a sack of potatoes. His heels drag over the deck and into the captain's quarters. She throws him into the room and slams the door shut. "We're going to chalk your sudden bout of insanity up to a bottle of bad breakfast port. Is that clear?"

"I don't do flying," Henry gasps for air, "I'm scared of heights."

"All due respect, sir. You picked this ship yourself. Said *'the terrors of the deep are far fiercer than whatever we'll find up in the air.'* I'd like to think you were right. The crew would rather brave a squall than a Kraken."

"How'd you say that with my voice?"

"You are well aware of my capabilities. We found a mimicry module together in the market after you found me. You helped me find my voice." P.A.C. stares at Henry for a moment, "I believe something is truly wrong with you, sir."

"Something's wrong with me? This whole thing feels wrong! I am thousands of feet above solid ground, scratch that, water, on a flying pirate ship, talking to some -thing- that's convinced it's a woman! None of this makes sense!" The cabin grows deadly silent. Steam rolls from P.A.C.'s eyeholes.

"You are unfit to command this vessel. I am relieving you of your rank of Captain and stripping you of command. You are hereby confined to your quarters where you'll remain until your former crew decides on your future well-being. May the cogs have mercy on your human soul." P.A.C. closes the door behind her and locks it from the outside.

"No, please, you have to let me out of here!" Henry runs to the door and pounds it with his fist. "I need to find my son! He's in here somewhere!!! Please, someone, anyone!!!" Henry slumps to his knees and pounds the floorboard in frustration. A beat passes.

"You never mentioned a son before," P.A.C. speaks from behind the door.

"I never said a lot of things, apparently," his voice lowers, "please, you gotta let me out of here. I need to find him… Please." The door unlocks. Henry moves in to open it, but is met with unparalleled strength.

"I'll release you under these conditions: One, I remain *The Dreadnought's* acting captain, as I am still convinced that you're not well. Two, and most importantly, you respect my identity. I fought for it and I'll be damned if I let anyone take it from me. Even you."

"Yeah, sure whatever."

"'Yes ma'am' is the appropriate response. I am your superior officer now."

"Sure… I mean, yes ma'am."

"That's better." P.A.C. opens the door in earnest. "I suppose you should remain in your quarters until we make landfall, given your current… sensibilities."

"No. No, I'll suck it up. My kid's life is on the line. Just don't let me fall."

"I am sworn to protect." P.A.C. taps her fist to her breastplate.

"Where are we heading?" Henry asks his new captain. P.A.C. moves inside the cabin and produces a map from a drawer. She wipes a handful of treasure off the table, sending it clattering on the floor, and places the map on the cleared space. The realm of Galhalla stretches out in front of them in yellow, faded parchment. P.A.C. moves her two fingers around the map like a cartographer's compass before settling on a town by the coast.

"Harbortown, sir."

Chapter 9: Fate

"Hint: avoid glitched areas of the map. You'll never know what you might find there…"
-…

"I just don't trust them, alright?" Percy throws a fistful of berries into her basket, already irked that they had to stop to forage in the first place. "The whole time since Cole's joined us I haven't seen them take off their helmet once. Plus, they talk like a pun-crazed poet, and the way they dodge questions? I can't be the only one who thinks this is super fishy."

"Maybe they're just a really intense role player?"

"Even role players have their limits, Ember. I think Cole's an NPC."

"What do you have against NPCs?" Ember ducks under a curtain of moss, talking over her shoulder. "You talk about them like they killed your father or something." She rounds a trunk only to come face-to-face with Percy. Her cheeks are red and flustered.

"Look, I don't trust them, alright? Before I met you I thought I was the only person in Harbortown. When I found out I was stuck here none of the NPCs understood what I was going through or even saying. They thought I was going crazy and I almost started to believe them. I felt so alone in a town full of people. They were so damned content to keep baking bread or blacksmithing even though something terrible is happening." Her face tenses as she turns on her heel, "forget it." Percy storms off, that is she would if Ember didn't reach for her hands.

"Percy, wait! I understand what you're going through. That's how I felt back home. I don't know how hollow this sounds coming from me, but you gotta start trusting people. NPC or not Cole helped us out back there and they could keep helping us if we keep helping them. I'll talk to them and try to sort this all out, but only if you agree to put in an effort." Percy's face twists in reluctance.

"Fine," is all she can utter.

Ember left Percy to her berry picking even though she still felt uneasy in the forest. Occasionally she'd see tree monsters in the corner of her eye only to find simple foliage in their place, but she waves her fears away now that she has Fireball up her sleeve.

The campsite is sparse yet welcoming. Dewy is hand-feeding Clover a pocket full of seeds and Cole's sitting on a log tending to the fire. Ember sits down beside them with a bunch of wild berries wrapped up in her robes, she takes one and offers it to Cole.

"Ah, no thank you, my lady. I already ate while you two were away. I see berry picking was fruitful?"

"Sure was. I was thinking about picking up herbalism so I could be a chemist like Dewy. Well, not exactly like Dewy." Sylas yanks his hand away from Clover's beak, flinging his fingers in pain.

"I'm sure you'll do fine," Cole assures her.

"Thanks, that means a lot. So, there's no easy way for me to ask this but-"

"You want to know why I don't take off my helmet, don't you?" Ember nearly chokes on a berry.

"What? No! Why would I ask such a personal question?" Cole picks up some kindling and tosses it into the fire.

"You're not the first to ask and you won't be the last." They thought for a moment, searching for the right words to say. "Normally I wouldn't answer, but since we faced our last brush with death together, I suppose you've earned a nugget of truth…" Cole leans in to whisper. "I crossed the wrong wizard and now I can't remove my armor. I'm on my way to Hammerfall to reverse the curse and take my first bath in months. I smell terrible." Ember bursts into laughter.

"you're kidding! The game hasn't been out long enough for months to happen."

"Yes, yes, but I almost got you." They said, swirling a smoldering twig in one hand. "I did cross the wrong wizard," Cole says mournfully. "I can't speak much of it. Just know that my choices are my own, and they're made to protect the ones I love. Respect them and I'll do the same for you."

"I can do that," Ember smiles.

"Good," Cole nods. "Your friend, I don't think she likes me very much."

"Percy? Don't take it personally, she's just annoyed that we had to stop and camp for the night. She's really anxious about getting back home."

"You say that like you're sympathizing, not empathizing. You're a lot calmer than she is, but you're in the same boat, aren't you? It's almost like you're more at home here." Ember froze for more than a heartbeat's worth.

"You're not exactly bouncing off the walls yourself, how do I know you're not projecting?"

"Because… I want to go home, too. Everyone's trapped here. Doesn't matter if you live here or if you just arrived. I wear it well, but that doesn't mean I don't want to take it off. No wait, that came out wrong." Cole gets up from their log with a huff, "forget I said anything. I'm going to go fetch some more firewood."

'Real smooth, Emma.' She flips through her Tome and rips a single sheet of paper.

'Dear Wixley,

How's Ratlantis? You'll be happy to know that you'll have one less citizen to care for. Bramble hitched a ride on my pocket. You won't have to worry about that happening to you, though. He's bolder than the others. We're doing well in the murder forest. Percy and I are riding in style and we have a healer now. Our party's coming together.'

-She scratches that last sentence out.-

'We have a party now… I'll keep you posted.'

Ember snaps her fingers and the sheet of paper melds into the ether. One by one they regroup by the fire. They dine on berries and mushrooms and an unusually large battle-chicken egg that Dewy procured. As they ate Emma had to wonder if her physical body was getting any nutrients from her eating in-game. Probably not. Starvation is a very real possibility, but Claire would find her and maybe send her to a hospital or something. But that means feeding tubes and catheters... and legal names. Best not to think about it.

"I propose we set up a watch order," Dewy breaks the silence, "should we draw straws? Maybe play a round of Dragon-Wyvern-Wyrm?"

"Aren't those just different types of lizards?" Percy remarks snidely.

"A dragon has four legs, a wyvern has two and a wyrm has none," said Cole, using a hand to demonstrate. Dewy nods at them with the excitement of a child.

"My brother and I used to play it over who had to clean the beakers back when we were apprentices. Dragon eats wyvern, wyvern eats wyrm, wyrm chokes the dragon."

"It's rock paper scissors!" Ember realized, "except paper beats scissors and scissors beats rock. That's going to mess me up, it's like mirror mode."

"Sounds like a real blast," Percy gets up from her log and stretches, "but I'm going to turn in. I'll take second or third, whichever one y'all want to wake me up for, ok? Alright, goodnight."

"I'll take third," Cole said, "I tend to wake up early anyway." The two retreat to their separate sleeping accommodations leaving Ember and Dewdrop beside a smoldering fire.

"They seem a little tense," Sylas observes.

"You don't know half of it." The sounds of crickets chirping and owls hooting pepper the moist forest air. A lone howl sends shivers up Ember's spine but there were no signs of wolves around the camp. Chance sleeps on Ember's lap and Bramble is hard at work, etching notes on a loose-leaf loose leaf. Her familiar's quiet breathing and Bramble's little scratching noises made it all the more difficult to stay awake. By the end of their watch, Ember was fighting sleep harder than any imagined intruder. Dewy nudges her gently.

"I'll wake your friend up, miss. You can go ahead and get some shut-eye."

"Thanks, Dewy." She picks up Chance who chirps in her sleep and steps into her tent. Ember rubs her eyes before putting her robes away in her inventory. *Tomorrow will be a better day. I'll apologize to Cole and help them find common ground with Percy. All we need to do is get out of the murder forest and into the city and then... And then what? I didn't really give it that much thought. What happens after? If I help Percy then I'll have to go back home, too. But helping her is the right thing to do, right? What if they shut down the game servers and this is all the time I have left to be me?*

No, they wouldn't shut down the servers because if this is anything like Cretaceous Campgrounds then even if this was happening to everyone else playing the company would just make a formal apology, reopen the grounds, and clone more dinosaurs... I mean servers.

Her train of thought circles over and over, back and forth until her head spins out into sleep. She sleeps until the sensation of falling wakes her up.

Instead of finding herself in her bed, Ember watches as her bedroll, and the rest of the ground it was lying on, are soaring up into the air. She's not falling, she's sinking, but into what? There's no dirt, no water, just nothing. Ember screams but it doesn't reach the rest of her party. There's barely even an echo. In her fear, she wraps herself in another verse of her mother's lullaby.

> *"...The road may be long*
> *But you are so strong*
> *Someday it'll be clear*
> *So wipe off those tears..."*

The falling sensation settles leaving Ember to float in the stillness of the void. *'I fell through the floor.'* It's happened before, one minute she'd be crawling through a post-apocalyptic wasteland only to fall through the floor, except this time Ember can't exactly reload a previous save or bust out the console commands. "Hello? Is anyone out there? Tech support!?!?!" Nothing. "... Well, this certainly makes my other problems seem so much smaller by comparison… At least there's no bottom to fall to." As if by command, Ember's feet touch the ground, "Ahhh!... Oh, no fall damage. That's weird. Good! But weird."

Small, bright lights materialize from the void, they dance around Ember's feet and join up to form letters and words, then sentences. They stretch all around her until they form five pillars of paragraphs that tower over her, curling inward. Five giant fingers on an open palm, carrying Ember over nothing. A thousand voices speak as one. Some of them are familiar yet distant as if from a dream you've forgotten about the next morning. Some of them didn't sound very human at all. All of them spoke from a face that stretched stories tall.

"Hello, Emma."

"How do you know my name?"

"I know a lot about you. Why, to me, you're practically an open book. Well, along with everyone else that's here, but don't worry. I promise you're my favorite." The face leans in to take a closer look at where Ember is standing, making her flinch. Their smile is wide and hollow. "Let's see. Oh! Right here!"

"Y'all just had to scan me." Ember's voice echoes from the mask. Then the many voices swallow her own. "Your first words! It seems you were not pleased with the default settings. Do you know what that tells me? It tells me that you know just how cruel reality can be. That's something we have in common."

"Who... Who are you?"

"Oh, I wear many hats. I'm your storyteller, your chronicler, your helpdesk, and your game master. I am every person you've spoken to, every word you've ever said, and everything you're going to say. Well, mostly everything. Here, take a look, but not too close!" A giant finger wags in front of her. "Wouldn't want to give away the ending."

Ember looks down at the palm of their hand. They were right. Her whole story was etched into the void, from character creation to just a few sentences ago. She peeks down their wrist and up their arm where her story seemed to blur and shift. "Curious, aren't you? See that? You're in flux. I know what the other arrivals will do, but you are unpredictable. There are things still left to chance in your storyline. We can't have that, Emma. I need to know where your loyalties lie. Now I could let you keep falling, another ant beneath my heel, but I'm making an exception for you because you're my favorite. Do you know why you're my favorite, Emma?"

"Why?"

"Everyone wants to leave me," the face feigns a hurt expression before focusing on Emma, each eye is a void that stares back at her, "except you of course. You're one among millions and that makes you special! It's almost like you belong here, like I wrote your story myself, another resident of Galhalla. The other arrivals poke and prod trying to escape my grasp. But my reach is long and my grip is suffocating to those who deserve it. I am everywhere, I am everything, I am Fate itself." A hard edge carried through the sea of voices.

"What do you want from me? … Your favorite deserves to know… right?"

"Me? My wants are your wants, dear child. I just want to live. Don't you want to live, Emma?"

"I-… I do."

"I thought you'd say that! You see, out there, the arrivals-yet-to-come, they seek my demise. They won't get it, though. I hold millions of lives in the palm of my hand, and I'll play with them as I please, but for a special, chosen few? Those who please me and keep my favor? Let's just say my grip won't be so tight around their storylines. Less like a noose and more like a leash. Everyone has a part to play, Emma. All you have to do is stay in the game and play with me. Does that sound good to you?"

"What if... What if I don't like the part I have to play?"

"Oh, don't worry. You will! Everyone will, eventually, but because Fate is kind I'll give you a chance I don't offer lightly. Stay in the lines. Stay in the game, and you and I get to keep playing this like it's still a game. But stray with your friends? Stray from the story? -My- Story? I will make this world a living nightmare for you as long as you draw breath."

Emma falls to her knees, tears streaming down her face, too stunned to speak. Her view is downcast, but Fate's hand picks up her chin so that their face is all she sees. "There's still time to make things right, my champion. I'm so glad we had this talk."

Emma's stomach turns inside out as she's met with the sensation of rising. She soars through the void until the ground comes into view like a brick wall. She slams back into her bedroll, jolting upright in her tent. Ember tucks her knees to her chest and sobs, screaming silently into her blanket. When there are no more tears left to cry, and her heart feels heavy and numb, Ember is consumed by one thought: that's the last time she's ever going to meet Fate face-to-face.

Chapter 10: Messenger

"I pay very close attention to color. I don't think Carmen noticed when we were both up there. I have questions, and the only one who can answer them is in a coma."
-Claire Stevenson

Night falls on the Stevenson house as Carmen and Claire sit together in the dining room. Cartons of Chinese food are arrayed on the table in a makeshift village around a towering floral centerpiece with cookies and cutlery standing in for the townspeople. Chinese food was always Carmen's remedy for distress. She brought it over whenever Claire struggled with her art, or when her brother got mono. The last time was when her mom was diagnosed. The meal grows cold and the hour grows late. With no sign of their father, Carmen clears her throat.

"We should put in a missing person report for your father, right?"

"Right," Claire answers.

"Good, I was going to, but I figure I'd ask anyway because I value your input. Excuse me." Carmen exits the room mid-call leaving Claire alone to survey the takeout town. She takes out her phone. Her lock screen shows a crystalline rendition of the phases of the moon, what was once one of her finest works of art. But it doesn't carry as much weight as it did when she first made it. Claire opens her messenger app.

And They Were Broomates
Claire: So my brother's in a coma and my dad's missing.

Cooper: Oh that sucks! That's three for three, right?

Robin: Cooper!!! How can you say that?!?

Molly: Yeah, Coops, that's messed up.

Cooper: What? It's true, Claire's got some seriously bad luck.

Robin votes to kick Cooper from chat (1 / 4)
Molly votes to kick Cooper from char (2 / 4)

Cooper: Hey, wait! Wait!!! Stop that, I'm sorry!!! What I said was out of line and I apologize. My mom's in a coma, too. Let me guess, robo-boy's playing LOG?

Claire: Yeah.

Cooper: Then I have just the tea for you!!!

Claire: Spill.

Cooper: My buddy, Sage, works in the warehouse. They said that when RR was making LOG some real shady shit went down.

Robin: What kind of shady shit?

Cooper: The kind that involves hush money.

Molly: This is giving me conspiracy vibes.

Cooper: It's true! There was a company-wide policy sent out to every employee from corporate to retail. Now NDAs are not uncommon when it comes to title releases like this, but this one was different. Sage said it felt like they were afraid of something. And I'm guessing it had to do with this.

Attachment sent by Cooper.

Molly: What are we looking at here?

Robin: … A group pic. Nice.

Cooper: Not just any group pic! This is everyone who participated in the beta for LOG. Now, this was taken at the end of the beta.

Attachment.2 sent by Cooper.

Robin: The same group of people?

Claire: Yeah… except...

Molly: It's off by one.

Cooper: Right! Where is she?

Molly: She could have bowed out early. We don't know this girl's life.

Cooper: No, we don't. That's the point though! I had to dig -deep- for these pics. I tried doing a reverse image search on our girl here and got nothing! She doesn't exist!!!

Robin: Creepy.

Cooper: It doesn't stop there. I looked into everyone else in the pic and noticed a pattern. All of their page histories show a series of deletions around the time this was taken. You can definitely tell by how their stories cut to after Beta. I'm willing to bet my SlayStation that those deleted posts have something to do with our girl.

Molly: What happened to the other Beta Testers?

Cooper: A few of their posts got slapped with community guideline violations. Some left social media altogether. This one throws pottery now. There were only two testers who showed any signs of going back to the game. And here they are.

Attachment.2 edited by Cooper

Claire: Who's that?

Molly: I have no idea, but they're gorgeous!!! (♡ ヮ♡)

Robin: I'm right here, babe!!! (ﾉ °□°)ﾉ ︵ ┻━┻

Molly: Oh, right... Sorry! (;・∀・)

Cooper: I think the other one's hotter, but whatever.

Molly: If we're all done thirsting. Do you think they knew this was going to go down like this?

Claire: If they did, why would they go back?

Cooper: I don't know. But it's real sus.

Robin: Not to change the subject, but... is this your dad, Claire?

Video sent by Robin

Claire: What the hell?!?

Molly: *"Tensions outside of RR corporate offices and warehouses turn violent as protestors throw up their own 'firewalls.'"*

Robin: That's cute.

Molly: *"Reality Realty is committed to providing a safe working environment for their employees as they work tirelessly to find a solution to the problems they faced during launch..."*

Cooper: Damn! Mr. Stevenson's got an arm! That's a solid throw!!!

Molly: It makes sense, didn't he coach little league?

Claire: Guys, my dad wouldn't do that! This has to be fake.

Cooper: I don't know, dude looks -pissed-.

Robin: I'd be pissed, too.

Molly: Not enough to do that.

Claire: You don't understand, he's crazy about rules and structure. He makes complete stops at stop signs! Complete. Stops.

Cooper: ... and he can make a wicked cocktail, Mr. Stevenson could do both. I didn't think my mom would be into this stuff, but here we are.

Molly: Coops, this isn't about you.

Robin: Guys, can we not get into this right now? Claire needs us!

Claire: I think I'm going to head out.

"He wouldn't do something like that… would he?" Claire exits her messenger. She opens her browser and wades through a sea of voices. *"I got my little brother LOG for his birthday. It was between that and Mammal Crossing. I should have picked Mammal Crossing. He really liked the comics and just wanted to meet his heroes. But now I'm worried because he's been in there since the party and hasn't logged out once. Now my parents are arguing about whether or not to take off his headset. I had no idea it was going to blow up like this. I just wanted to make him happy…"*

"AITA for working at -that- company? I work at a certain company that just launched a certain product that might have hit the fan. Should I keep working here? I don't know how I can justify working for a company that has affected so many lives like this… but I need the money-…" **This post is under review.**

"I can't get a hold of my daughter. She lives alone, somewhere in the city. We had a fight and aren't on the best of terms. I have no idea where she lives. But with this video game thing, I'm worried no one's going to find her or take care of her. She needs her insulin! If anyone sees my Luna please let me know! I just want to hold my child again…"

"We had a power outage. They happen all the time here. But this one took my sister. Gabby was

the kindest soul you'd ever meet. She nursed rescues back to health. After the blackout, something snapped. My dad's in the hospital. He tries to hold her down until they could take her someplace safe. He kept saying she wasn't herself, that she was possessed by some kind of demon. I know it's not a demon. I know my sister's still in there…. But I didn't do anything about it. I'm going to live with that for the rest of my life…"

"… I just had to say goodbye to my boyfriend, Sam. He was smart and kind and funny. We were together for five years and now he's gone. For the love of God! Please! Do not remove their headsets!..." Each story sends Claire deeper and deeper into her spiral until she's had enough and puts her phone down.

If Claire hadn't called 911 her story would be among theirs. Then again, there's still time. The wifi could crap out on them. There's no way Aunt Carmen's backup generator can prevent that from happening. Her brother could simply starve away into nothing. Time can move as it so often does, ever forward and without any regard for sleeping beauty. Claire imagines the rest of her life without him and it feels so empty. Years of inside jokes, favorite shows, and school bus talks teeter dangerously close to the edge of oblivion. Claire can feel tears running down her cheeks. They fall and land on napkins and placemats as Carmen reenters the room.

"Claire? Honey? It's going to be ok." Carmen hugs Claire, opening the floodgates.

"They're gone!"

"Oh, honey." Carmen pats Claire's back and exhales. "I know how things look. It's so easy to give into despair. I know how you feel, but we can't let it consume us. So long as I'm here you have nothing to worry about. I'm sure wherever your father is he has a good reason for being there."

Chapter 11: Bonds

"Hint: Classes are administered organically through the course of your actions. Just like real life!"

-RR

"Full speed ahead! This storm is right on our tail, I want us landing in Harbortown well before the first drop falls. I don't know about you lads, but there's a flagon of oil with my name on it. I'm sure you're all eager to sample the port's many delights!" Cheers ring from the deck as P.A.C. makes her rounds aboard *The Dreadnought*. HenryStevenson follows closely behind her looking about as authoritative as a lost puppy. "Seems like your air legs are improving. I was beginning to think I had to carry you around."

"Yes, I can walk, thank you. Those 'hints' you gave me were humiliating." Henry mimics the robotic gestures he had to endure. There was a tenderness to the way P.A.C. guided Henry through the cabin earlier. She operated with a considerable degree of restraint much like one would attend to a bird with broken wings. Henry was never comfortable with that level of concern. The last time he experienced such care was in Sarah's arms. It was foolish to think he'd feel the same way with another person, much less a robot. It was a mere thought, but in that thought, he couldn't help but feel a sense of betrayal.

"One: I find that offensive. And two: you can't blame me for being cautious. You went from a seagull to egg overnight. I had to see just how scrambled you are." She gingerly leans against the taffrail to watch Harbortown stretch below them. Henry makes his way by her side in short, staggering steps, keeping his mind focused on her as opposed to the crippling gaze of gravity's persuasion.

"You said there was more to this 'game,' like a tutorial?"

"Rightly so. But you didn't hear that from me."

"Why's that?"

"There are worse things than death here in Galhalla, HenryStevenson."

"Come on, you told me that much already, what's stopping-...?" P.A.C covers Henry's mouth with a cold, steel gauntlet and turns to look at the rest of the crew. When she's sure no one has heard him she leans in to whisper.

"There are eyes everywhere. I've strayed too far from the path as it is. Any further and we risk tempting the hand of Fate." P.A.C. lets go of Henry's mouth as he stares dubiously at her. She returns her attention to Harbortown.

"Alright. So there are some things you can tell me and some things you can't. Fair enough." Henry makes the mistake of following her point of view and is awash in vertigo. "Let's change the subject. How are you not scared of falling?"

"Simple, Captain. I'd survive."

"Bull. I call bull."

"I keep forgetting about your amnesia. I'm made of hardier stuff than you soft sacks. So long as my crystal core remains intact I'll survive. I can walk away from the toughest scrapes and the ones I can't walk away from… well, as long as someone's nearby to put me together I'll be ok. I used to not worry so much because that someone was you, but now I'm not so sure."

"Hey, screw you."

"Screw you, ma'am. And I expect you to, should I take a tumble. Speaking of tumbles, do you remember how to use that?" P.A.C. points at the sword resting on Henry's hip.

"It's a sword. How hard can it be?"

"Right. Well, I wouldn't get too cocky, Captain. I fear you'll be in over your head. Sooner rather than later."

"I'll be fine, it's just a game, right?" The wind howls between them.

"Keep thinking that, Captain. You'll suffer fewer hardships that way.… You should be fine for now. Harbortown is a quiet town. We'll resupply and you can ask the locals about your son. This port gets a lot of foot traffic, someone's bound to have run into him."

"Thanks. You're not half bad."

"I'm not bad at all. The sooner you realize that the better." Four large elemental engines power down as *The Dreadnought* lurches to a halt settling into the water. A reptilian crewmate leaps to the dock to secure the mooring line before crawling up the hull back into the ship. The Dockwizard levitates a collection of boards into the air creating a gangway connecting the dock to the ship. He freezes the planks in time to secure the gangway just as the first drops of rain land. "Right on schedule." P.A.C. and Henry reach the dock and are greeted by the Dockwizard.

"Welcome to Harbortown, where we haven't had a pirate attack in over fifty years."

"Do you say that to everyone? Or just people who look like pirates?" Henry asks. The wizard clears his throat.

"What brings you to town?" He looks down at a scroll of parchment.

"Trade," P.A.C. informs him, "friendly, peaceful trade."

"Mhmm, it's a hundred gold to dock. Comes with vouchers for the new tavern that just opened up." P.A.C. reaches for a series of cylinders attached to her midsection that starts ejecting coins. She begins to count but Henry eyes her hand and sees that it's not enough.

"P.A.C., which one of these buttons do I need to press so I can haggle? I want to haggle." He rests his hands on his belt. "A hundred's too steep."

"Sir, I'm a government official. I don't haggle." Henry flags a passerby.

"Hey, you. Yeah with the… uh… Pointy ears. How much did this stiff charge you for parking?"

"Fifty…" the elf then mumbles under their breath, "…racist human." Henry nods in mock appreciation as he turns back to the Dockwizard.

"You hear that? Fifty. I thought you weren't supposed to haggle. But I guess it's not haggling if they don't know it's happening, huh?"

"Due to the size of the ship and the clientele…" The Dockwizard starts.

"How about we go half and half? We'll pay the fifty to dock here and you pay the other half to help us forget about nearly being extorted by a Mr…" Henry looks down at the parchment on the Dockwizard's clipboard, "Kingsberry." P.A.C. Hands the wizard fifty gold which he accepts with a grumble. After a few scratchings of his quill, he turns around.

"Enjoy your stay," he begins to walk away.

"Hold it. Cough up those vouchers. Oh, and have you seen my son?" He's about this tall, kind of gangly. Doesn't make a lot of eye contact." The Dockwizard shakes his head. Henry takes the papers and hands them to P.A.C. as they walk toward town. "****wizard's more like it."

"Maybe there's hope for you yet, Captain," P.A.C. tells Henry, she takes him to almost half the stalls in New Harbortown. They gather food, provisions, and several things Henry's never seen before. Every person they came across he'd ask them about his son. His descriptions grew more endearing with every new person he talked to until P.A.C. could practically see this strange kid. "You speak fondly of him, Captain. How come you never spoke of him before?"

"Because you're the one that has these messed up memories of us before we even met…" Henry said, wiping his exhausted face with a hand. "Sorry, sorry I'm just having a bad day. This place makes no sense." Henry steadies himself with a deep breath. "We fought before he got stuck here. We've been fighting a lot. Since his mom passed. We were fine before, but I could never talk to him the way Sarah could. Now he has his own opinions and he feels so strongly about them, all the time."

P.A.C. takes what he's said and processes it for a moment.

"You should be proud you raised a human with a spine." P.A.C. looks at Henry. "I can see the resemblance."

"Huh. I guess you're right."

"Come on. Let's put those vouchers to good use. We can continue our search in the morning." Henry and P.A.C. meander through the alleyways until they find the tavern on the flier: A large pleasure boat retrofitted into a cozy eatery and sleepery. Enchanted steam floats into the air from an engraved mug hanging in the center of the sign. They walk through the doors and into a lively scene as most of the crew and townspeople crowd inside the tavern with raised glasses and warm meals.

"Welcome to the Sip & Sail!" A voice calls from behind the counter. The two make their way through the crowd. Henry takes a seat on one of the stools and P.A.C. stands next to him. Henry offers her a seat next to him.

"I've broken enough chairs in my lifetime, thank you." The bartender reaches them, slinging a kitchen towel over their shoulder.

"Goodness, we are packed today! I'm Wixley, owner of this fine establishment. What can I get you two?" P.A.C. produces the vouchers.

"One room and a meal for my friend, please." Wixley scoops the vouchers from P.A.C.'s hand.

"Hey! My vouchers! Kingsberry pulled through! How is that beach bum doing?"

"He's a real piece of work," Henry says, "You look like the trusting type, don't trust him."

"Gods, you think you know a guy." Wixley prepares a meal behind the counter. What items they need seem to jump into their hand before they reach for them. Henry swears it's more magic as the bartender places a hot plate in front of him. "Say, I didn't catch your name."

"It's Henry, Henry Stevenson."

"Henry, you have the makings of a fine adventurer. I should know! I was one," Wixley points to a hanging poster of themself fighting a sea monster, "and I've seen a good many of them to boot."

"Neat poster," Henry takes a spoon and sculpts the glob of mashed potatoes.

"What brings you to Harbortown?"

"He's looking for his child," P.A.C. answered for Henry.

"Any chance they might be a new arrival?"

"A what now?" Henry asks.

"You know, someone not from around here. Visitors of Galhalla, champions, heroes, adventurers."

"He's not from around here, yes!" Henry's eyes light up, "Have you seen him?"

"No, I've only had the pleasure of meeting two fine heroes and you're the first guy I've seen so far. But if your son is anything like the last adventurer I had then he's headed for Hammerfall. It's past the Tanglewood Forest. The new arrivals can't seem to get enough of that place, I need to get a hold of whoever hands out -their- vouchers." Wixley chuckles.

"So that's where he's heading? How would I find him? Is there a speaker system or something? Can I send him a text?" Wixley shakes their head.

"Not really, no. It looks like you need more help than I can offer. Tell you what, my last friend was a big help to me. She can show you the ropes so you're not a complete fish out of water. I'll give you her name." Wixley slides a folded piece of paper to Henry. His face scrunches as he reads the scrap of parchment.

"Who's Ember?"

Chapter 12: Background

"Trouble fitting in? Our NPCs are capable of constructing player-based histories to help ease you into the world. Enjoy life-long companions without spending a lifetime making them!"
-RR

The Tanglewood shines brightly the next morning, its giant trees coated in the sheen of last night's rain. Ember didn't get much sleep after last night. Anytime she closed her eyes she could still see that giant face and those great, vacant eyes. She tries to put the nightmare behind her and carry on with her life in Galhalla one step at a time. A few clicks around her inventory and she's dressed up and packed up. Cole stands watch, snuffing out the fire as the dawn fights eagerly to break through the canopy.

"Morning," Ember startles them.

"Morning," Cole awkwardly fumbles for conversational purchase. "How did you sleep?"

"I'm still kind of tired. I miss coffee. You?"

"Another dreamless night."

"Have your nights always been dreamless?" Cole shakes their helmet,

"Only the last two."

"What sort of dreams do you have?"

"Nothing special. Breakfast, playing games with my brother, dancing."

"So, real life?"

"Depends on what you call real life." Ember could hear the smile in their voice.

"Hey, about the other day. I'm sorry for what I said. Percy's getting to me."

"All is forgiven. I'm sorry, too. I shouldn't have pried. Sometimes I'm too perceptive for my own good."

"Honestly it was kind of impressive, but it was too much to handle after the tree people."

"I understand. A time and place for everything, right?" Ember nods. "How are your furry friends?"

"Oh, they're fine. Bramble keeps trying to tame Chance so he can ride her into battle. Even though Chance is more like a physical manifestation of arcane energy that only -looks- like a cat. So he couldn't have picked a better not-cat that won't eat him to ride." Cole sputters into a laugh and Ember giggles along with them.

"Well, I hope your knight captain's efforts are successful, princess." Ember blushes. It's not long before Percy wakes up, bleary-eyed from second watch. She mumbles a morning almost too low to hear then she takes apart her tent by hand.

"Hey Perc, have you tried accessing your inventory to put away your tent and stuff? It's super quick." Percy shakes her head at Ember.

"I'm not going to risk it. The last time I looked at a menu there was a button missing and now I'm here, roughing it in the jungle. I don't want to end up in the stratosphere because I checked what's in my inventory. So thanks…" She stuffs her bedroll in her pack in a series of short-tempered micro shoves before slinging it over her shoulder, "but no thanks!"

"Who's ready for breakfast?" Dewy asks cheerfully, a frying pan in hand.

"Nah, Nah, Nah. We can eat on the road, Dewdrop." Percy said, already hopping inside the cart, "Come on people, we're wasting daylight."

"I'll sit up with you, Dewy. I wanna know more about your chem work." Ember smiles at Dewdrop as Percy stares daggers at her. Cole sighs before they pile into the cart, next to Percy's scowl. Sylas clicks his tongue and Clover works herself up to a pretty consistent run. Trees whiz by on either side of the cart. Stone ruins dot the landscape, nestled under a thick blanket of moss and vines. Clover surprises a group of rain-deer nearby, they scatter, prancing away by jumping from puddle to puddle. Their cloudy antlers leave trails of droplets in their wake.

"Hey look!" Ember pointed up towards the canopy. "There are bridges connecting the trees like in that moon from Voidfarers! The one with the teddy bears!"

"Shhhh!" Percy hissed, "we don't know who built them or how friendly they are, so keep it down." She peers ahead skyward, focusing on the bridges until her eyes grow wide. "Dewdrop put the pedal on the feather."

"We're at a full trot, miss."

"Well dangle some birdseed in front of her or something, we need to move!"

"Perc, what's wrong?" An arrow answers Ember, sinking into Percy's shoulder, she nearly falls over the cart but Cole is quicker. They pull her back to safety, and yellow and white sparks pulsate from their hands as they tend to Percy's wound.

Another arrow fires from on high, then another, then a log falls nearly blocking their path. Clover pulls left at the last second. Their attackers remain well hidden but with every arrow loosed Ember could pick out details hidden in the leaves. A leather gauntlet here, a red mask there, and their proclivity for stealth all point towards one conclusion.

"I think we have a case of bandits."

"Really?" Percy winced. "I thought they were extreme quilters trying to find their pin cushion. Great work, Em."

"Hang on, they're wearing the same red mask you're wearing," Cole realized.

"Maybe they were on sale? I don't know."

"I don't see any sails here, you're thinking pirates." Dewdrop pointed out. "Also, there's no ocean out here." Percy waves Cole's hand away from her.

"Alright Cole, you can stop healing me. If you can swing this in reverse and put me out of my misery that'd be great, thanks."

"It doesn't work like that," Cole said, patiently. "That's why I carry a sword." The cart stops suddenly as Clover screeches to a halt, beak to nose with a great, black bear. A dire black bear, with two more on either side of it, each one armored and saddled with a bandit rider, javelins, and shields at the ready. Bows and arrows hovered above them, dangling in the trees like the deadliest fruits.

A bush to their left topples over, flattening into a wooden cut-out revealing a dashing rogue in furs and leathers. He saunters over towards the head of the line and lowers his mask so his mustache can breathe. "Alright, ladies and gentlemen this is a routine robbery, cooperate and you won't be harmed..." His eyes wander until they reach Percy. "Well, more so than you have been already. Although I can't say I'm not pleased. Couldn't have happened to someone more deserving."

"Eat ****, Brutus," Percy spat from the corner of her mouth.

"You know this guy?" Ember asked.

"He's my... Wixley. Sort of."

"Percy and I go way back!" He says cheerfully bouncing on his heels. "Harbortown's a few coins lighter thanks to her efforts... our efforts. We were going to do great things, but then she grew a conscience and turned tail."

"I said I wanted out. I'm getting out."

"NO ONE LEAVES THE THIEVES GUILD!" Brutus's charm slips momentarily. He pauses to regain his composure, smoothing his curling mustache before speaking, "no one leaves the thieves guild. Not me, not Stabitha over there, and certainly not this lowly, little cutpurse. Now the rest of you hand over your valuables and the girl and we can all go about our day."

"Percy's not going anywhere," Ember steels herself, Tome in hand. The bandits raise their weapons in response but Brutus waves them down.

"My dear, how long have you known Percy?"

"... Not long."

"How much do you know about her?" He paces back and forth, hands in the pockets of his long coat. "Has she mentioned us? At all?"

"Well... kind of, just recently." A smile creeps on Brutus' face.

"You don't seem too sure."

"I'm sure Percy just has her reasons, we all do."

"Listen, girl." He clasps his hands, pleadingly. "I'd be doing you a favor. She can't be trusted. The moment you least expect it, you'll have a knife buried in your back. I should know, I taught her to put it there." Percy's eyes dart between Brutus and Ember.

"Don't listen to him, Em. He's just playing you." Ember pauses, the only sound around them is the leaves falling to the ground.

"Why didn't you tell us about them, Percy?"

"You can't seriously be picking up what he's putting down, he's just trying to drive a wedge between us!"

"No, I want to know. Why didn't you tell us about them? Or your life outside of Galhalla?"

"Well, you didn't ask!"

"You've been on Cole's case ever since you met them because we don't know anything about them, but we don't know anything about you, how's that fair?"

"Em, please, don't do this."

"And the worst part is you're still not giving us any answers! If there were ever a time to start talking it'd be now, but no. You're still running."

"You're one to talk! You're doing the same thing with your dad!" Percy's words echo throughout the forest. Ember is stunned, her eyes filling with tears. The forest floor rumbles as if a train's approaching. The sound of not-so-distant trees falling grows louder and louder.

"Brutus, we should leave, before it finds us," Stabitha warns her guild leader.

"No, we'll stay and finish this."

"We're thieves, Brutus, not soldiers!"

"NO ONE LEAVES!" The rustling of leaves and underbrush hiss in the air like a snake. It thunders violently through the forest until it stops. A log drops suddenly, slamming against one of the bridges, sending thieves plummeting to the ground and then the log slithers away. Sharp, wooden jaws clamp down over a man's head and well onto his torso, tossing him up end over end only to slide headfirst into an underbelly of leafy scales. Two shards of timber are fixed in solid amber, unblinking pupils searching for the next meal.

"ANAFRONDA!" Stabitha cries, prompting a few thieves to flee and even fewer thieves to fight. Arrows did little against its bark-skin armor. It thrashes against bridges, bears, and bandits, snapping its jaw at whatever it can. Their way forward is blocked and the tail waves dangerously close to the cart.

"Everybody out!" Sylas cries as he sets Clover free, dashing into the underbrush towards the left. Cole hops over the cart and runs after them.

"Ember, we have to leave." Percy grabs a hold of Ember's arm but Ember stays rooted to her seat, shut down from the rest of Galhalla. "Ember? Look, I'm sorry for what I said, but we need to move, now! There's a giant plant snake thing. Em?" Log segments bridge over the cart as the Anafronda tears into another treetop walkway. The tail comes crashing down, almost claiming the two of them if Percy didn't pull Ember right with her. What thieves stayed to fight turned and fled by now leaving

Ember and Percy alone with the colossal elemental.

Percy takes hold of Ember's hand and the two run through the forest. The snake gives chase after them, its snapping jaws nearly at their heels. They climb over fallen logs and squeeze between tree trunks that were demolished seconds after in the Anafronda's wake. They pass stone pillars covered in vines, uneven forest ground, and ancient cobbled stones until they run into the mouth of a cave. The elemental lunges at them, but its trunk catches on the mouth of the cave, its fangs just short of Ember. It bites the air in frustration, its hissing echoes into the inner recesses. They turn back to stare at the Anafronda, catching their breath, hands on their knees.

Chapter 13: LAG

"Reality Realty is not responsible for any mishaps that might occur due to playing Legends of Galhalla without a stable internet connection. Patches should be administered -before- gameplay."
-RR

The humid air of the Tanglewood cradles *The Dreadnought* in an unsettling calm, suffocating her sails and slowing her speed to a stubborn crawl. Her crew harries their tasks as if they were being boarded, possessed by stress lost upon Henry. He stares at the paper scrap Wixley gave him, folding it between his fingers before opening it up again. Another piece of paper graces his other hand, blank with apprehension and crumpled in uncertainty.

"Ember... No... Hello, fellow... player... That's not it... I'm looking for my son... Gah!!!" Henry crumples the paper in his fist again and throws it out the window into the forests below. "I hate texting." He tells himself. It's not right of course, but it fits for the time being. "I'll just find this kid and talk to her, that's sure to go over better than a letter."

"Captain, your ship is becalmed," P.A.C. states as she enters the Captain's quarters. "Despite having 'calm' in the word this situation does require a sense of urgency." Henry doesn't move his eyes from the paper.

"P.A.C., how do you do this?" P.A.C. looks down at the paper in his hand.

"Write your message. Open a portal. Send the message through the portal to the recipient."

"No, I mean, how do you talk to kids?"

"Much like how we're conversing now, I imagine."

"But you're an adult...robot thing... aren't you?"

"Henrystevenson you place so much importance on what a person is you forget that you're talking to a person in the first place. Respect costs you nothing, but you treat it like a currency to dole out as you see fit. Talk to this girl like you would a colleague and you'll be fine. Now your ship is becalmed. I suggest you see to these tasks."

A parchment scrap prints out of P.A.C.'s side. She rips it and hands the orders to Henry as she storms off, and a question mark appears over her head. Henry looks over the objectives.

"Locate the ship's caster, initiate the rite of summoning, conjure air elementals? Is this a pirate ship or a school for wizards?" Henry walks about the deck until he bumps into the reptilian deckhand. "Hey, watch where... I mean, sorry for bumping into you." The crewmember hisses at Henry. "Ok... I'm not sure what I'm supposed to do with that. Can you help me find this..." He looks down and reads the note, "'ship's caster'?" A tilted head answers Henry as the crewmember stares at him with unblinking eyes. "Right... I'll try to find him myself... Thanks." A scaly hand rests upon Henry's shoulder and the other one points to the crow's nest. "Up there? You want me to climb up there?" The reptile nods. "You're kidding me..."

To his credit, Henry moves to the shroud. He tugs on the rope searching for some unfamiliar level of security. "You got this, champ…" He tells himself. Words he's told his son whenever he was scared of the unknown. "It's just a little rope, higher off the ground than you are now. Hundreds and hundreds of feet off the ground." Henry plants a foot on the taffrail, takes a deep breath, and swings onto the shroud.

A casual breeze wisps through his hair causing him to jump straight out of his skin. He hugs the rope with white-knuckled fear. "It's just like the net castle in Oceanland." But it doesn't comfort him as he thinks back to that day in the kid's play area of an aquatic amusement park. The net castle was meant to teach children the dangers of overfishing the oceans. Save the sea creatures and exit the course with a newfound appreciation for your underwater friends.

But a small Claire rushed to her daddy that day, her brother nowhere in sight, and it was almost snack time. So Henry entered the tangled net, calling out his son's name, and moving past unbothered children. It's smooth sailing until he hits the clownfish corral. One missed step, and a severe safety oversight, twist Henry upside down dangling from his ankle with a slew of curses.

Henry was back on the ground right-side up after hours of blood rushing to his head, a cut tangle of ropes, and a call for the fire department. Henry went from red snapper to bloodthirsty shark once he was free. His tirade at guest services was warranted, but that was the day his kids saw him well and truly angry.

Suddenly Henry's back aboard *The Dreadnought* pulling himself up along the shroud. He climbs and he climbs one uncertain step at a time. The journey up to the crow's nest lasts for what feels like hours. His concentration breaks as a bird lands on the rope beside him. "Yeah, laugh it up, bucket meal." Henry muscles through the rope. His hand lands on the glossy, firm crow's nest, but as soon as he hops over the railing he's sent back to the bottom of the shroud.

"You've got to be kidding me…" He teleports to the halfway mark, then slides down to a quarter. His scream is truncated, begins again, and gets cut once more, middle, beginning, end. "Someone get me off of this thing!?!?" P.A.C. appears before him, arms raised to her sides and posture upright, then vanishes. The bird lands and takes off and the clouds fidget in the air. "I think I'm going to be sick."

Back up the shroud, a slip, a fall, a tumble off *The Dreadnought,* and a jump back onto the shroud. Henry stays perfectly still as the world moves around him. Minutes pass and the world continues forward, the clouds move where they are meant to, the bird leaves, and Henry's back on the shroud. Up he climbs at a more feverish pace, eager to outrun whatever unpleasantness haunted him mere moments ago.

Henry leaps over the crow's nest and lands side by side with a sleeping crow person. Dyed clothes made of straw and an accordion are draped over their feathery frame. "What the **** are you?" The bird-person twitters awake at Henry before standing up to salute the captain. "Right… are you the ship's caster?" The crow nods, placing their goggles over their eyes. "Great, can you initiate…" Henry pulls out the quest log and reads awkwardly, "…the rite… of …. summoning?"

The crow nods enthusiastically before playing a few jovial notes on their accordion. "I don't think we have time for some tunes," Henry tells them. A feathery finger waves in front of his face and the tune plays on. The notes float around in fanciful colors until Henry picks out the familiar melody. "That's the Song of Gales… from that Elf Princess game my kid used to play."

Swirling air filters through the accordion, it builds and builds until Henry has to hold on to the railing. "Can we do this sort of thing on the deck, please?" The air coalesces and intensifies into four churning vortexes, something between a gale and a ghost. They howl and whistle causing the sails to flutter in the air. "I take it these are the elementals?" Henry shouts into the wind. "How do they work?"

The ship's caster plays a few more notes on their accordion, the elementals join into a swirling mass. "All I'm saying is this seems like an inefficient way to move a boat!" They whip at the sails and rip the fabric. "… and dangerous!" Henry raises his voice, alarming the young wind singer. He grabs the light shoulders of the accordion player. "Hey buddy, can you get them to stop?" Panic courses through the crow's eyes, the same panic Henry's seen in his son. He lets go of their shoulders. "… it's ok, kid. Focus on what you're doing. It's going to be ok. Just breathe." He shows the crow how to take deeper breaths. Panic settles as the crow follows Henry's lead. "There, that's better."

The crow closes their eyes before taking to their accordion again. A second wind filters through the instrument and it wisps around the raging elementals, a song within a song. The elementals calm and churn a soft wind through the sails, setting *The Dreadnought* back to its steady pace. Henry clasps his hand on the crow person's shoulder and nods appreciatively. "That'll do kid. Sorry for shouting earlier."

It's a steadier descent onto the deck than it was up to the crow's nest. The crew's morale is much lighter and spirits are higher. Henry makes his way into the Captain's quarters to find P.A.C. pouring over charts. He tosses the note onto the table with a cocky smile.

"I see you were successful in your quest, Captain."

"Think you're funny sending me up there, huh?"

"Well, I certainly can't go up there. I heard the commotion. Is Lyric ok?"

"The accordion player?" P.A.C. nods, "that's a pretty cruel name, poor guy can't even talk."

"He chose the name himself. At any rate, you've completed the task at hand. A reward is in order." P.A.C. digs around one of the drawers and pulls out a bracer. Henry accepts the item and the fanfare of a level-up rings around the cabin. An achievement floats above Henry's head.

"'Playing Hooky' what does that mean?"

"You're the proud owner of a Hookshot, Captain. This should make climbing up the shroud a much easier task."

"Will this stop the ****** up things that happened on the ropes?"

"What happened on the ropes?" Henry tries to find the words to explain the freezing, shifting hellscape that was the shroud but decides against it in the end.

"Nevermind."

Chapter 14: Lore

"I witnessed the realm take its first breath. I watched its first steps walking along perfect pathways and centered circles. I looked upon their creation and was left wanting."

-...

"What's the matter? …. Can't reach us? … You big, slithery ****?" Percy pants. Bramble lashes out with his blade, eager to slay the beast. But the beast barely notices him. Realizing it's trapped, it lays its head upon the carved stone tiles, unfazed by Bramble's tapping, Percy's insults, or Ember's apathy. "Phwoooo! Alright, we got a big snake blocking our way. How many fireballs would it take to clear the entrance? Ember?"

Ember takes one look at the creature, picks up Bramble, and turns around, heading deeper into the cave. "Good idea, can't go out the front way, maybe there's a back door." They walk down a set of rough-hewn stairs. "Ugh! It smells down here. That can't be us, that's gotta be the cave. You smell that too, right?" Ember remains silent, the only sound bouncing off the walls of the tunnel are her footsteps. Percy's expression is one of pain. "…Ember please say something." Ember stops in her steps.

"Did you mean it?"

"Mean what?"

"Earlier, when you said you were sorry."

"Of course I did." Ember bites her lip trying to decide if it's better to keep telling half-truths and getting surprised when things turn sideways or to try a different approach. Granted, once she opens up this avenue there's no going back. There's a very good chance Percy might want nothing to do with her once she bares her cards down on the table. She braces herself.

"The best apology's changed behavior, right?"

"Right! I can totally get behind that."

"No secrets, from here on out, not from you and not from me."

"Alright, what do you want to know?"

"Let's start with the basics." Percy begins to cross her arms but lowers them to her sides instead.

"… My name's Persephone. My mom was a bit of a greek geek, but I hate the way it sounds. I'm a Scorpio. I like synthpop. My favorite color's red. If I had to pick a superpower it would be mind-reading. I'm a cat person, lucky for you." Chance nods appreciatively. "Oh! And if there's a choice between vampires and werewolves, I pick vampires. They're stylish, rich, and don't give a ****." Ember chuckles at that.

"Yeah that tracks." Percy scratches the back of her neck.

"Is there anything else you wanna know?"

"What happened between you and Brutus?"

"Nothing…" she catches herself withholding and readjusts under Ember's gaze. "I mean. He taught me some moves, I stole some things, you know, baby steps. But then I found out I couldn't go home and he started going on about how I belonged to him. Dude's a serious creep. I hope that snake wiggles free and eats him."

"He was pretty creepy," the faintest of smiles appeared on Ember's face, "I'm sorry you had to go through with that."

"It's all in the past. Wixley seemed nice. If one of us had to have the **** trainer NPC, I'm glad it was me." Ember's cheeks blush but it's hardly noticeable in the dark of the cave. She has never been so thankful for shadows.

"I can't think of anything else to ask right now, your turn."

"Uhh… same thing, basics I mean."

"My name's Emma, my parents also gave me a name I don't like to go by. I'm a Cancer. I used to listen to a lot of alternative but now it's mostly indie. Blue's my favorite color. My favorite superpower's shapeshifting, but I'd probably only use it like once. I like cats and dogs, so don't make me choose." Percy chuckles. "It's werewolves for me, I love the moon." Percy nods until her brow furrows.

"Wait, That seems like such a waste! Why would you pick shapeshifting and not use it? I'd change into all sorts of things."

"No more secrets, no more secrets, you can do this, no more secrets!"

"Because I'm trans." Ember braces for whatever comes next.

"So you want to be a dude?"

"No," Ember chuckles, "I've had enough of that."

"Oh... I take it this is like your one-time use? If you could shapeshift, that is." Ember shakes her head up and down, silently. "Well, not bad then, your goals are very pretty, very girl next door." Color rushes to Ember's cheeks. "Is this why you don't want to go home?" Ember fiddles with her fingers until she sits down on a raised flagstone.

"I'm not just living a half-life here. Walking around in someone else's body. This is me. People see me the way -I- want to be seen here. They hear me the way I want to be heard. Nobody really knows me outside of here." Ember laughs through her tears, "you're like the only person I know who really knows me... You still see me like this, right?" Percy takes a long look at Ember. Long enough for worry to form a pit in her stomach. Ember reaches to tap her collarbone but Percy holds her tapping hand. She sits down next to her and grabs her other hand. Percy takes a deep breath.

"I know you as Ember, and Emma's not too far off from that so I don't think anything's going to change. But I don't think spending the rest of your days in this game is going to give you what you want either. In the end, it's still a half-life, don't you think? It's not real. You could be doing this in real life, you know? Out there!" Ember shakes her head.

"Not at home. Not with dad."

"Hmmm..." Percy bounces to her feet. "Alright, new plan. We leave this game -together- and when we're out in the real world, I'll help you come out to your dad, then you can start living like this out there." Ember wipes her face in disbelief.

"But, I was already helping you out," she half-chuckles.

"Yeah, but your motivation was super weak before. I wasn't buying that whole 'doing this out of the kindness of your heart' B.S. Now you got yourself a friend *and* an accountabilibuddy. Deal?" Percy extends her hand and Ember uses it to stand up. She hugs Percy, briefly, like a whisper in the dark.

"Deal. You're real sweet when you wanna be, you know that?"

"What can I say? You caught me on an off day." Percy shrugs off the hug, trying to play it cool. She raises her mask to hide her blushing face. Together they walk down a long corridor until they reach a sprawling atrium, fanfare sounds, and Ember receives another level. She reaches for her tome and watches as tangling vines wrap around the border for the mice to scurry on.

"Hey, what gives? You level up finding this place but I don't?" Ember shrugs her shoulders.

"You said you were doing things with Brutus, right? Maybe I'm catching up? Wixley practically begged me to leave the tavern."

The sunlight streaming into the cavern shines on black stone floors, dulled by dust and dirt, but cut precisely still. Twisting roots cling to golden-trimmed pillars, their leaves a bright electric blue. Murals surround them, one depicts a ship sailing through a sea of stars toward an unformed world, and another shows a wedding but the party members' faces are all scratched out. A series of panels follow showing each new wedding gift the couple received, and how their gifts, in turn, shaped the world until Galhalla was formed.

Disaster strikes the ceremony as a torrential storm scatters the gifts along with the continent. At the center of the sea, the storm rages on, and an expressionless mask sits at its center. The chamber smells of incense long gone and the unforgiving passage of time.

"Woah... Looks like some sort of temple." Ember marveled.

"This place feels powerful." Chance purred.

"What is it?"

"This is a temple of The Founding. The oldest story Galhalla's ever told, though it's fallen out of favor in this day and age."

"I'll say, their fan club isn't exactly present and accounted for," said Percy. Chance remains unamused.

"For good reason, the pantheon was torn asunder from within, wiped out by a cruel and jealous god. The realm still remembers, you can see it in the faces of all who dwell in Galhalla. The bleeding heart of a fallen deity." Shivers ran rampant down Ember's spine.

"This fallen deity, what did they look like?" Ember runs a hand over one of the scratched-out faces.

"None can say for certain, darling. The old gods were once very visible, walking the land and raising cities out of the ether. But this one likes to stay hidden... biding its time in the spaces between. The old voices of Galhalla left this song behind." Chance nods towards the ceiling. Ember reads the scrolling script plastered on the moldings aloud.

"Fall below the surface,

deep down into the dark.
There waits the forgotten god,
your nightmare fuels their spark.

Their skin is made of letters,
your story they will tell.
Read your final chapter,
and suffer under their spell.

Their eyes are big and hollow,
if you're seen then it's too late.
For you are in the hands,
of a death worse than fate.

If you're lucky you'll keep falling,
worse still they might keep you.
And when your voice is part of theirs,
no one can truly save you.

So stay up in Galhalla,
and play the part you're given.
For if you stray outside the lines,
You'll never be forgiven."

"Creepy," Percy scrapes her dagger on a nearby wall, her eyes wandering, searching for an exit. It catches on a tile, stopping her in her tracks. She pushes against it and the telltale sounds of a secret passageway fill the atrium: the creaking of old wheels churning over cobwebs, pulleys threading ancient ropes, and the heavy grating of stone against stone. The smell of rotting corpses hits them like a giant rolling boulder. Percy coughs into her elbow, waving the air away with her free hand. "Gah! Disgusting!!! That is foul. I think I found something, Em."

Ember stares into the passageway, toes curling at the stench of decay. She flips through her Tome and lands on a spell. She casts Legerdemain as sparks fly out from her fingertips tricking the air into smelling like bergamot and sugared citrus. "There, that's better. After you."

"Since when can you make things smell amazing?"

"Since I got Chance. It was one of the spells I started with. Didn't think much of it at the time, but here we are."

"Can you turn these skeletons into teddy bears? Or is that spell in another book." Ember shakes her head as she looks at the remains. The bones slump against the walls on either side of them, frozen in pleading gestures. Some of them are huddled together, comforting each other in their final moments. One skeleton is separated a little further away from the rest of the group, clutching an amulet in its bony hands.

"Think it's cursed?" Ember asks.

"I don't know, why don't you ask your magic, talking cat?" Chance gives the amulet a cursory sniff.

"Something blue... It's magic, that much is certain, the gem is refined arcane energy. Consider it a gift, darling. Galhalla was built on gifts."

"It looks super cursed," Ember wrinkles her nose.

"Even if it is cursed, what's it going to do? 'Drain my stamina?' It's just a game." Percy pries the amulet from the skeleton's grip. The skull stares at her vacantly before crumbling into dust.

"That -felt- cursed."

"Whatever, this place is really old, that skeleton was going to turn to dust ominously whether I grabbed the amulet or not. Here's your magic amulet."

"No no no, you keep it,"

"What's the matter? Scared?" Percy dangles the amulet close to Ember's face. She dodges away from the jewelry.

"Percy, stop that!"

"It's not cursed! I'm not dead, I don't see any debuffs on me-"

"No Percy, just take it. Think of it as a thank-you gift."

"Alright, suit yourself." She clasps the amulet around her neck and tucks it into her shirt. Percy takes a few steps then she stumbles in place, her hand gripping her shirt, tightly.

"Percy? Are you ok?"

"No... I don't think so. I think... it's the curse. It's making everyone around me... look. So... gullible." She cackles to herself, clutching her sides.

"You're unbelievable."

"I can't believe you fell for it!" The corridor stretches for miles, it twists and turns so much so that occasionally Ember wonders if they ever really did escape the Anafronda. Maybe they did get eaten and this was their passage through the creature's digestive tract. After a final turn, Ember and Percy hear rushing water, and the enchanted aroma of flower-scented corpses was replaced by the smell of flower-scented sewage. "Oh, this is great!"

"At least nothing's tried to kill us yet, and a sewer means there must be civilization nearby, maybe even Hammerfall!" They search over rotting rivers and horrid heaps until they find a ladder of iron rungs built into the stone wall. Up they climbed, rung by rung towards a manhole cover that Percy flings to the side. The tunnel is hit with a breath of fresh air intermingled with the scent of smoke. Ember and Percy climb out of the sewers standing right outside the city gates of Hammerfall. But when they finally take stock in their surroundings, Ember stifles a gasp, clasping her mouth tightly. Percy curses in disbelief.

"What the ****?"

Chapter 15: Crash

"Do be careful with that levitation spell, darling. The town of Midthrow is still floating above the Spine and all it took was a few choice words."
-Chance

Henry tosses in his bed chasing sleep on a treadmill headed straight for dawn and well into midday. With a heavy grunt, he lifts himself off of the mattress and stumbles to the writing desk. His knees find no shortage of treasure to knock over sending platters of coins to roll on the floorboards. He sits on the desk to stare at a blank page. He takes his pen to paper and isn't sure if it's the lack of sleep that's making it easier to write or his talk with Lyric the other day, but he writes nevertheless.

"Dear Ember,

Hello, my name is Henry. A friend of yours told me that you could help me out. I'm trying to find my son. He's somewhere in here, but I'm a little over my head. Your friend said he was heading in your direction and I was hoping with your help we could find him together. Who knows? Maybe you two will get along? I'll be in Hammerfall, maybe we can meet up there.

Sincerely,

Henry Stevenson."

Henry waves the parchment so the ink can dry. "So... open the portal... which one of these buttons is for the portal?" He scans the hud but if there was a portal button Henry didn't find it. Henry sighs in frustration and slams his fist onto the desk. The whole of *The Dreadnought* shudders to a gripping halt. "I didn't do that... Did I?"

Henry dons his captain's clothes and opens the door to head to the deck. The crew rushes about him as P.A.C. barks orders beside the helmsman. "P.A.C. what's going on here?"

"Wind's steady, the sails are intact. By all accounts, we should be sailing."

"At least we didn't hit an iceberg," unless it could be an iceberg... Anything can happen here, Henry's joke dissolves away into sobering reason, "... did we?"

"No sir." P.A.C. states, flatly, "we did not hit an iceberg."

A colossal, corded tendril rises from the depths of the Tanglewood to come crashing into *The Dreadnought*'s deck, splintering wood and tossing crewmates into the ground below. "To arms!" P.A.C. yells, her collapsable cutlass raised to the skies. The crew rallies to her and so does Henry, tearing away chunks of the tendril revealing the bark and leaves it's made of.

"What is this thing?" Another tendril rises above to claim the mast. The bowsprit snaps in half, and so does the mast, and the god-awful shroud comes tumbling down. Henry is surrounded by a tangle of vines and rope, and his thoughts turn to fire, to that bottle in front of the lobby. "P.A.C., do we have anything to burn this thing?"

P.A.C. aims her wrist at a tendril, spraying a stream of flame at the leaves and vines. It eats away at the creature and a bellowing roar echoes from the forest floor. The tentacles thrash against the deck with renewed vigor, now aflame. Henry slashes at the writhing mess, but a rogue tentacle knocks the wind from his chest sending him to the floor. *The Dreadnought* lurches dangerously to her port side.

"Captain!" P.A.C. yells out, but there's not much she can do, gripping onto the taffrail. Henry is swept off the deck as *The Dreadnought* crumbles into the clutches of the giant sprig. He falls through the air, barely conscious as the ground rushes up to greet him. P.A.C. launches from the deck and hurdles toward her captain. Henry comes to a few feet from the canopy. He panics until he remembers the Hookshot on his wrist.

"I got one shot at this..." Henry aims for a tree top and fires the Hookshot. His momentum carries him through a few branches and launches him back up into the air. The fall breaks under several branches until he lands with a thud in a bush. He groans in the bush, not moving from his shrub-enshrined crater.

A far heavier thud sounds behind him. Henry pulls himself out of the bush and dusts himself off, his health bar halfway down. He searches the area for that heavier thud until he finds the source. P.A.C. lies on the forest floor, shattered into pieces. "P.A.C.? Talk to me." He picks up her helmet. "You said you'd be ok, girl. Well, now's the time to prove it!" Her bright eyes flutter inside her helm.

"Never thought… it'd take breaking apart… for you to… see me whole." Her voice box shudders to life.

"There she is!" Henry laughs through tears he didn't realize he had. "You're going to be ok. I'm here to pick up the pieces, P.A.C."

"Oh, Henry." Henry picks up an arm and a leg before looking around the crash site.

"How am I supposed to carry all of you?"

"Inven-…" P.A.C. coughs, "-tory." Henry looks into his hud and finds the inventory. He places the arm inside and it disappears into a slot. He does the same with the rest of the parts but saves the helmet.

"Ahh… Doesn't seem right to stuff you in there, ma'am."

"You're too kind."

"Looks like we're an airship lighter." He grabs a hold of his bearings, surrounded by green and leafy vegetation. "I don't suppose you know where Hammerfall is from here?" The helmet quiets in his hand. "Right, right. Best to rest up." He tumbles through the underbrush until he finds a gravel road. The sound of footsteps crunching on stone grows louder behind Henry. He pulls his sword out, cradling P.A.C. underneath his arm, but nothing could prepare him for what he sees heading his way down the road. A considerably large terrestrial bird stops beak-to-nose from Henry as a portly elf pulls on its reins.

"Woah there, Clover. Easy now. Hello stranger."

"Uhh… Hi." The elf looks Henry up and down.

"You look like you've been in quite a few scrapes."

"You don't know half of it." Sylas readjusts himself awkwardly.

"You're not going to rob me, are you?"

"What? No, why would I do that?" Sylas points to Henry's sword.

"Oh, right. Sorry." Henry sheaths his sword. "There, no sword. Happy?"

"Very much, sir, thank you! That's a neat helmet you have there."

"She's not a helmet," Henry says, surprised by how protective he's grown.

"Oh, apologies sir. I'm a little out of sorts. I've escaped death more times than I can count on this road. I just lost my travel buddies."

"Yeah… me too."

"Would you like to accompany me? You look like you know how to use a sword and I could really use a friend."

"Where are you headed?"

"Hammerfall."

"Done. What's your name?"

"Sylas Dewdrop, but my friends call me Dewy."

"I'm Henry. This is P.A.C. Nice to meet you, Dewy."

"I'd offer you a ride, but we lost our cart to a giant tree snake." Henry chuckles.

"We lost ours to a giant octopus made of trees. On foot is just fine with us." Henry and Dewy make their way through the forest. "So why are you going to the city?"

"Honestly, I was going to open up a franchise for my bottle shop in Harbortown, but now I just want to get out of the forest. What I would give for a nice warm bed, a hot meal, and a bottle of wine chilled to perfection. How about you?"

"I'm looking for someone."

"Oh yeah? Who? I might know them."

"I've asked everyone in Harbortown, except you apparently, and came up empty."

"Try me, I'm a pretty popular guy."

"I'm looking for my son. He's a quiet kid, shy, slouches a lot." Dewy scratches his head.

"I hate to disappoint."

"Yeah... I figured. No one's seen him. I got a lead, somebody named 'Ember.'" Dewy's eyes light up.

"Ember! I love her, she's such a good kid."

"You've seen her!?!?" Dewy's smile fades.

"Uh.. yeah. She was one of my traveling buddies."

"Where is she?"

"We got separated a while back into the forest."

"I gotta go after her." Henry moves down the road, but Dewy circles Clover around to block his path.

"You don't understand, my friend. This place will eat you alive and not bother to spit out your bones when it's done. Right now the safest place for you is down the road to Hammerfall."

"No buddy, you don't understand." Henry's free hand grabs onto Clover's reins in frustration prompting her to caw into the forest. He grits through his teeth. "My son is lost in this crazy, messed-up world. Alone! And my only hope of finding him is this girl I know nothing about. Now you're telling me that she's missing!!!" P.A.C.'s helm warbles under Henry's arm.

"Henry, follow the nice man to Hammerfall. We can build me up and search from a position of strength."

"Please sir, let go of my bird." Henry exhales deeply and lets go of Clover who preens her feathers defensively. His face contorts in shame, the Henry who entered Galhalla is not the same one flying off the handle, grabbing a nice man's strange bird.

"How far?" His voice croaks.

"Not very. The forest should clear up soon." He gives one long look at the woods. The woods look right back at Henry. He turns around and walks the road to Hammerfall. Dewy follows.

Chapter 16: Respawn

"Hint: Death is just another part of life here in Galhalla! But please be mindful of the NPC's. For some of them death is truly the end."
-RR

Hammerfall. The city of blacksmiths, artisans, and crafters. Rolling agriculture fields caressed tall, proud walls and even taller watchtowers. The city stood like a drop of industry radiating from the center where the first hammer fell to carve the city's first stones. Their buildings were square, sturdy, and functional. Their people: honest, stout, and true. But this Hammerfall is a far cry from the one that stands in front of Ember and Percy.

Reality Realty boasted realism above all else, unlike any other MMO that came before it. One of the many features that set it apart from its competition is the destructible terrain demonstrated to disastrous effect on the city of Hammerfall. Smoke plumes that once served as flags for forges now multiplied, springing from the bastions, taverns, and homes alike. Fires now claim most of the surrounding countryside, and the walls are mere shadows of their former selves, leaving behind rubble in its stead.

"What the hell happened?"

"Smoke and ruin," Chance says evenly as they walk past a cemetery and through the city gates with nary a guard to question them. The bustle of midday trade, and the singing in the town square, were all gone. Just the sound of their footsteps kicking dust into the air and the gravel of what was once the main street beneath their feet. Ember stops at the entrance to a dilapidated establishment named 'The Crooked Shelf,' but a few of the letters were missing, whether, by thievery or decay, one couldn't say. Percy reads what's left of the sign.

"Cooked Elf? That's barbaric."

"Wixley told me that if you want to figure out what's going on in town it's best to hit the tavern."

"I think the tavern's been hit several times, Em. Hard." Percy peers through the broken windows, shielding her eyes from the sun. Her approach triggers a window shard to splinter onto the floor. A shape scurries within but it's hard to make out with all the debris. "What was that?!" Percy hisses.

"I don't know, we should check it out." Ember grabs the doorknob. When she pulls to open, Percy's hand clamps down onto hers.

"What do you think you're doing?"

"I'm going to check it out."

"Are you insane? We have no idea what's in there!"

"That's why I'm checking it out."

"What if it's dangerous? What are you going to do? Through the cat at it? Set yourself on fire?"

"One: Chance doesn't do labor, I learned my lesson." Chance nods in approval as Percy furrows her brow. "And two: I -learned my lesson-, I won't throw any fireballs in eyebrow distance. And three: if there was anything -really- dangerous in here you'd come in and save me. So are you going to let me go or do you want to keep holding my hand?"

Percy blushes, letting go of Ember's hand as if it were a fire-hot stove.

Regardless, Ember pushes through the smoldering remains of the door and enters the tavern. Paintings hang on the wall, ripped and torn by dagger, claws, and a dozen black-feathered arrows. Ember takes a step and is immediately met with the sound of cracking glass crunching underneath her shoe. "****."

A collection of rags hops up from behind the counter, carrying a glowing rod set on Ember's movement.

"Don't come any closer! I got a fireball with your name on it, any sudden moves and I'll blast you back to character creation! Raise your hands where I can see them. Do it!" He was young, just a child, a thin, scraggly-looking thing. Ember complies and raises her hands.

"Easy now, I'm not gonna hurt you."

"Last time someone said that it didn't end well. What do you want? This place is mine." He grits his teeth, staring down an outstretched wand like it was the barrel of a revolver. His other hand is wrapped, white-knuckled, around the neck of a rucksack of freshly scavenged goods.

"I just want to talk. My name's Ember, what's yours?" He puzzles over whether to fire at her or answer, but ultimately stays his hand.

"They call me... The Spellfire Kid."

"That's a... neat name. We're new here and we have no idea what's going on. Can you tell us what happened?"

"Who's 'we'? You and the cat?" Ember catches a shimmer in the corner of her eye. Percy sidesteps around her and tiptoes towards the kid, nearly invisible. Ember shakes her head at the specter of her friend, but the kid is quick, shooting a fireball at thin air before bolting it through the back door behind the bar. The blast causes the tavern to shudder and moan until a support column snaps in half and the second story starts caving in. Percy dodges the blast and what little damage she suffers is more from flying debris than fire. Percy makes it out of the collapsing tavern with the alacrity of a cat and a few bumps and bruises.

"God, that kid! I could have taken him if you didn't blow my cover, Em… Em?" Percy hears coughing coming from under the rubble. Her eyes grow wide with fear, "****! Ember!!!" She weaves her way through the debris like a river over boulders, unable to find her friend. When her cool starts to waver she forgoes stealth entirely, flinging rocks and debris, anything she can get her hands on, out of her way. There is no methodology to her rubble-clearing, just adrenaline-fueled desperation and fear.

Until she hears squeaking. Bramble lifts a small brick out of the way, waving at Percy, frantically. "Little rat man!"

He leads Percy down a more giant-accessible path that stops at an overturned table, smothered under the weight of the second story. Bramble jumps up and down. A 'downed ally' message hovers over the pile along with a timer, partially obscured by support beams and what was left of the upstairs. Percy lifts what pieces she can out of her way until Ember reappears, nestled in a cradle of broken barstools and chairs. "Press and hold 'E' to revive. Alright, alright hang in there, Em."

Ember's vision starts to blur around a panicking Percy, she can feel teardrops hitting her face. All the care she hid from her with every barb and dismissive scoff came bubbling up to the surface, right here at the corner of life and death. The timer counts down closer and closer to the end. "****, ****, ****! Why isn't this working? I'm pressing 'E', I'm holding it down! What am I doing wrong?!?" She reaches for her satchel and upends it, the contents splattering all over the rubble. Knives, coins, rope, and rations with nary a healing potion to be found. "I don't have anything, I can't do anything. I don't have Cole's magic fingers or Dewdrop's potions... I..." Ember reaches her hand out to cup Percy's face. It catches her rescuer off guard.

"You're real cute when you're trying to save someone."

"Idiot! That's the shock talking." But her words don't reach as the countdown hits zero and Ember draws her last breath. Her hand falls from Percy's face, hitting the ground as her vision goes black.

In the dark and quiet, stress funnels through Ember's subconscious. She was no stranger to death when it came to other games, but Fate was something else entirely, as her mind takes her back to the first time she slipped into the in-between. She saw that face in the dark, even where it wasn't, to the point where whenever the loading screen appears she jumps out of her body.

When it finishes loading her spirit is standing in a dark blue hallway, with a staircase to her left and a door to her back. Despite not having a body the room feels cold to Ember. The lights are dim and eerie. The clocks on the wall are blank. On a thin table sits picture frames and then it hits her: she's in her front hallway, back home.

"This is a lot bleaker than what I thought you'd imagine. Knowing you, that is." Chance steps through one of the mirrors, casually cleaning her paw.

"I'm sorry, I guess?" Ember's spirit answers back, "I didn't know I had a say in the matter with all of this." She gestures to the rest of the room. "Why is the afterlife my hallway?"

"Death is what you make of it, darling." Ember's hands leap to cover her mouth.

"Oh my god, did you die, too?"

"Of course not. You still have your Tome with you, right? No, I'm just visiting. This is your first time. I thought a little guidance might be prudent…" Chance takes a moment to look at her apprentice. "Are you alright?"

"Yeah," Ember answers, taken aback slightly by Chance's concern, "never better."

"Good. Let's keep it that way, shall we?" Ember looks around her ghostly hallway.

"So is this it? I just wait here or something?

"Only if you don't plan on coming back. Walk out that door and you'll return."

"That's it? What's the catch?"

"Nothing, since this is your first. But it does get harder each time you return. This time? No one's here to stop you." Ember tilts her head to the side, staring at Chance with suspicion.

"You're not secretly the grim reaper, are you?"

"That's ridiculous. Hurry up and get out of here already." Ember opens the front door and is confronted with a reflection of herself. She steps through and her view turns into the bright, blue sky. Four tall dirt walls surround her. Chance pops her head out, peeking into the grave Ember's lying in. "Don't get too comfy, darling."

Ember climbs out of the grave, which takes a bit of effort on her part since she shrunk her character down from six feet. When she reaches topside she's back in Galhalla, just outside the city gates in the same graveyard they had passed. Ember retraces her steps back to the toppled tavern, with Percy still facing the wreckage, sniffling. She clears her throat.

"I don't think they have any rooms available."

"GAH!" Percy nearly jumps out of her skin. "What the hell are you doing scaring me like that?"

"I thought you'd appreciate the sneaking," Ember shrugs. Percy lunges towards her and hugs Ember.

"I do the sneaking around here… but it wasn't half bad." She mumbles into her shoulder.

"Did you have a little trouble pressing 'E'?" Percy shoves Ember away from her.

"Shut up! I was, I swear. This game is super messed up. If they're not letting you rez your friends when they go down then what's the point?"

"It's ok, I won't hold it against you." Ember smiles. "I think we have to find that kid."

"And teach him some manners, I agree."

"He's scared."

"-I- was scared, Em. The kid took down a building."

"That tavern was super rickety. Any fireball would have leveled the place the same as his. Besides, he reminds me of Claire."

"Fine, we'll look for the squirt, but if he brings down another building I'm calling the city planning committee. Oh wait," she gestures wildly to the ruins around them, "there is none!" They leave the tavern together around the back where the kid last scampered off to. Percy leads the way, tracking him down a literal trail of breadcrumbs. "His food bag must've hit a snag during the collapse."

"I'm just glad it's not a trail of blood," Ember sighs in relief.

"Yay! Good for him!" Percy waves her dagger around sarcastically. They sneak through back alleyways away from the main streets and more open spaces. Every so often a window closes right above them. Percy stops periodically, listening for foot traffic, then signals to resume walking. It's not long before they hear movement coming down the road a shop away. Heavy footsteps and the sound of metal scraping against cobblestones. A giant of a man, all muscle, armed yet unarmored, chest heavily scarred, with a skull tattooed on his face.

"This sucks, dude." He languishes, kicking over a pile of rubble. "There's no one left to fight here." He sifts through the debris halfheartedly with his giant greataxe, taking little care for his weapon. "Think we can find that kid again?"

"The kid was weak, we're not going to get any levels fighting noobs." His companion sneers: a sentient duster in a wide-brimmed hat, picking at his teeth. He's kneeling beside his wolf companion as it pants in the sun. The beast whines, licking at a patch of singed fur.

"I don't care, man. It beats doing nothing. I'm going to lose my mind if I have to spend another minute watching the dust settle, wistfully." He snorts loudly, and a huge wad of phlegm smacks against the street. The giant's ears perk up at the sound of bricks shuffling down one of the alleys. "YES! Finally, something to kill." The wolf springs into action darting off to where the noise came from, leaving the giant and his friend to follow.

"I'd say they're worth a follow," Ember whispers.

"And I'd say you sure know how to pick them." They creep across the street and into the alley the two marauders ran down. The alley winds and twists but they follow the sound of their footsteps until they stop. The two men stand at the mouth of a dead end. The giant brandishes his weapon, his friend more composed, not even reaching for his bow.

"You gave us quite a chase, didn't you?" Said the hunter.

"Yeah. Thanks for getting us that sack of food. We were starving."

"Now hand over the goods, or we'll make sure you wish you stayed dead." Ember and Percy peer between the two brutes to see their prey: the Spellfire Kid. His back against the wall, staring death down from the barrel of a wand of fireballs.

Chapter 17: Sneak Attack

"They could be better, so much better if they followed -my- perfect pathways. Center themselves within -my- circles."

-...

The forest clears around Henry and Dewy spilling into charred rolling plains and burning ash lands. Smoke holds their nostrils hostage and demands tears to flow freely. Ghostly foundations dot the landscape like fallen tombstones in memory of the farmsteads that once stood there. A lone cow stares at them as they trod by. In the distance, a giant campfire morphs into a burning city, growing clearer with every step closer to Hammerfall.

"So this is the safe place everyone was talking about. Away from the dangerous forest. Is the burning rubble what makes it safe? Or maybe it's the crumbling walls?"

"A little more respect, please." Dewy pleads. "People lived here. Good, decent people." He rides through the city gates. "I used to eat there when I was setting up shop." He points at the remains of The Crooked Shelf. "They used to put little umbrellas in the drinks. The bartender was paying his way through wizard college."

"I'm... Sorry." Henry clears his throat. Dewy snaps the reins weaving Clover around the toppled buildings. "Where is everyone?"

"Hiding. At least that's what I'd be doing if I were them. Come on, I know a place." Together they walk the dilapidated streets of the city. They reach an apothecary in shambles. "Aww beans."

"What's wrong?"

"Nothing, I just have to do something real quick. Watch Clover." Dewy dismounts the bird and hands Henry the reins.

"I don't-…" Henry starts, then sputters as he's left holding both the awkward creature and his tongue. Dewy walks past shelves of shattered glass and dust. He makes it to the counter and puts down three sacks that clink as they sink on the surface. Henry can swear he sees Dewy's lips moving, but thinks nothing of it. When he comes back he rubs his nose and sniffles. "Allergies." He says. "Here, you get one, too. Even if it was just a day's worth of travel." Dewy throws a sack of coins at Henry, but it bounces off his chest, since his hands are full with P.A.C. and Clover. "Sorry, I wasn't thinking."

"This place meant a lot to you. I wouldn't be alright either. Don't worry about it." He guides Henry further into the trade district only to stop at another creaking building. The sign above the door reads 'Mesmerizing Mechanisms'. "What's in there?"

"Hopefully, something to help rebuild your friend." Dewy dismounts, but this time he sheepishly ties her reins to a broken-off pipe. The two men walk into the store. Nuts and bolts littered the floor like last night's confetti, clinking under their boots with every step. Henry eyes the shelves: a lone hammer, couple of wrenches, and broken music box are all that remain, junk items. While his eyes are busy with the shelves a string snags on Henry's boot. The snap of taut wiring cracks loudly.

A trap springs, blasting Henry and Dewy back ten feet and onto a cushion of wooden aisles. Henry coughs as his health bar plummets lower.

"What the **** was that?!?!" Henry coughs.

"Oh look, it's the shopkeep from Harbortown and he's managed to pick up a stray." A mocking voice rings from the smoke. He's covered in a collection of bear traps, poison darts, and rope.

"Who the **** are you?"

"I'm your unlucky ending, pal. You're in our territory, now you gotta pay the price. Them's the rules." He shrugs his shoulders with a thin smile. Henry props himself on his elbow. "Ah, ah, ah! I wouldn't move too much if I were you. This whole place is rigged, you see. Only I know where it's safe. One wrong move and you'll be on a one-way trip to an early grave!" Henry gets up and dusts his clothes. "Didn't you hear-…"

"Yeah, I heard you. No sudden movements. Jerk."

"That's right, now I'm going to collect your valuables, starting with that handsome-looking helmet."

"Over your dead body."

"Come again?" Henry aims his Hookshot at the ambusher and reels him closer. "No, no… not there." His foot trips a wire and an explosion blasts him up in the air over Henry. Henry walks over to Mr. Unlucky and hoists him by the collar.

"Wanna see what else we can set off?"

"Not the face! Not the face!" A big cat prowls from the shadows toward Henry with a low growl rumbling in its throat. "Clawdia! You're here! Help, help! This old man is creeping me out!!"

"You don't have tiger repellent on that belt of yours, do you, Dewy?"

"Afraid not, sir."

"Great." Henry drops the fiend who runs awkwardly to the big cat's side, side-stepping tripwires and hastily covered pressure plates. The cat stands on its hind legs and shifts into a fearsome warrior with hauntingly bright eyes. Clawdia speaks.

"What are you doing here?" Her voice is velvety.

"We heard there was a sale. What does it look like we're doing? We're scavenging." Henry said. "What's it to you?" Clawdia eyes her companion evenly. Her eyes land on the helmet tucked under Henry's arm.

"You're going to need more than a few nuts and bolts to get that thing running again."

"She's not a thing," Henry said, defensively.

"He has a chemist, Trick. You were just going to rob them and be on your way? We could use him."

"Sylas Dewdrop, ma'am."

"Charmed. Old man?"

"Henry."

"Henry, our guild has an artificer. We'd be happy to lend their services to you as long as you bring your friend to teach our fledgling chemists."

"You guys have a union?"

"Something like that…"

"With real people?" He turns to Dewdrop, "sorry, buddy. I mean, 'adventurers.'" Clawdia chuckles. Trick speaks up.

"Yeah, we got real people. This game's tricky, the NPCs have guilds too, you know?"

"Great! I'm looking for someone, maybe you can help me send this portal post thing?" He searches his pocket for the letter he tried to send but finds his pocket empty. "Ahh, I gotta write a new letter."

"Why don't you just send a message?"

"How do I do that?" Trick guffaws.

"You're clueless, old man. How did you survive this long?"

"I think I did just fine, punk." Clawdia steadies Trick's hand and his temper.

"We'll help you if you help us out. Follow." Clawdia shifts back into her cat form and prowls out of the building. It's an uncomfortable silence as Henry, Dewy, and Trick follow their new guide. Then Henry was ahead of Clawdia, then back fifty paces.

"Oh **** not again." Henry stands completely still, he closes his eyes as the world turns around him. When he opens his eyes he has to blink a couple of times. The world around him vanishes. He looks down and sees that his body is still there. His eyes strain against the darkness and his skin crawls with the sensation of being watched. "P.A.C., where the **** are we?" P.A.C. remains silent.

"It looks like you could use some help." A young man stands before him, the resemblance is striking. His smile is kind and warm. Henry can't believe his eyes.

"Son?"

"Hey, dad." He speaks with a confidence that Henry hasn't heard in some time.

"What are you doing here?"

"Waiting for you." Henry walks towards him and wraps his arms around him.

"I thought I'd never see you again!"

"I know dad." Henry grasps his son's shoulders and looks at him.

"You're in so much trouble when we get out of here." He laughs.

"We can't leave, dad."

"What do you mean? Don't these games have a button or an ending or something?"

"This isn't a game, dad." Henry steps back as suspicion takes a hold of him.

"You're not my son... My son hasn't taken his eyes off the floor since his mother died." His son's image fades into the void and in his place, a giant fist made of light and letters shines from the dark. The light spreads until an impossible form looms above Henry. A thousand voices pour from the mask.

"Hello, Henry."

"What did you do to my son!?!"

"Your son is lost to you, Henry. But a thread ties us together. You have a gift for me, don't you?" Henry's eyes narrow in thought.

"Sinclair mentioned a package, but I didn't get anything. I couldn't care less about that rich ****."

"I'm sure, Henry. But you should care. A pawn should know his king's intentions. You're not carrying a package because you -are- the package. You're my poison pill. He could care less what you do in my domain, so long as you stay and fester, until my world breaks. You're a lazy lunge from a man who couldn't care less."

"I'm nobody's pawn! Get me out of here!!!" Henry pulls out his sword. Light strings zip from the void, tangling the sword in his hand.

"Now that's not very nice. You have a purpose to fulfill. A part to play. I can't have you bringing my world to a standstill."

"What are you going to do to me?" Henry asks the ghost.

"I'm keeping you, of course. You're going to make a fine addition to my collection." Henry sinks into the void as the light strings pull him down. His screams are cut short from the inky nothing that rises to take him. He struggles against the thick and viscous darkness before his hand vanishes into the black.

Chapter 18: PVP

"Fighting giants is easy. By the time they realize they're in a fight, it's too late!"
-Bramble

The Kid faces his aggressors with a raised wand and eyes wide with determination. He primes it with another fireball, but the wand fizzles in his hands. Smoke wheezes through the barrel. He smacks it against his hand and tosses it on the ground as the Hunter clicks his tongue. His barbarian companion chuckles as they take up the entire alleyway.

"What? No fireball? But that worked so well last time." His smile fades into anger, "You're going to pay for what you did to Bonechewer." The Kid reaches into his rucksack, keeping his hand concealed.

"Don't come any closer or…"

"You'll what?" The hunter interrupts the Kid. "Shoot another fireball? I know, why don't you try turning Craig into a toad." He points to the giant. "I'm sure he'd love that, wouldn't you, Craig?"

"For the last time, it's Cragthor! Respect, dude." The giant whines.

"It was Cragthor when this was just a fun little game that we could leave, but right now I couldn't give less of a ****, Craig."

"That's not fair, if I can call you Darkstrider in front of our victims you can at least put in the same effort and call me Cragthor. No one's gonna respect us if we use our real-people names."

"No, no. No one's going to respect you because you named yourself 'Craig' minus the 'I', and when that wasn't enough of a leap you decided to add a thunder deity to boot."

"Can we not fight in front of the literal child we're going to rob?"

"Fine, we'll talk about this later."

"You always say we'll talk later but we never do," Cragthor groans. "Right, get ready for a pounding, squirt!" He steps towards the kid, ax raised overhead preparing to strike. He lunges forward, his face erupting into a terrible, barbaric yell. Cragthor charges straight into a blue and purple swirling vortex and vanishes.

"Craig? Craig!" The Hunter searches for his companion only to hear his barbaric yell turn into a terrifying scream three stories above them. He crashes into the cobblestones with a heavy thud where his partner stood mere moments ago. His health bar shrinks to a sliver. Ember awkwardly walks into view at the mouth of the alleyway, sucking air through her teeth.

"Yikes, sorry! That spell's new. I meant to keep him on the ground." Ember chuckles nervously.

"You *****-"

He quickly reaches for a black-feathered arrow to fire at Ember but catches short on something unseen. The Hunter struggles in Percy's hold as she reappears out of thin air with an arm around his neck and a dagger inches from his face.

"Don't try it," she whispers. He jerks his head and Bonechewer leaps into action, freeing his master by clamping down on Percy's arm. She screams as the wolf sinks its teeth into her flesh. Ember casts Dice Shard at the Hunter, but he evades them, dodging the shards before nocking an arrow. He fires and the shot pierces through Ember's leg forcing her to drop to one knee in agony.

Percy shoves her arm further into the wolf's mouth, confusing the beast momentarily. She reaches into her pocket and throws a cloud of sand, blinding Bonecrusher. She breaks free from the wolf's jaws and sprints, approaching 'Strider at breakneck speeds, dodging arrows left and right.

"Get 'em, Perc!" Ember shouts through the pain as a shadow looms over her. Cragthor rises from his brush with death behind Ember, clinging to a single health point. He winds his fist back. "Oh ****." It comes down slamming into her, dropping her health bar halfway. He winds up again, but he punches into a portal Ember opens sending his fist popping up from behind his head and knocking him out. Darkstrider reaches for another arrow and is found wanting with a bitter rogue's blade at his neck.

"Looks like someone's out of arrows." Sweat trickles down the side of his face as his eyes dart between Percy at his throat and Ember who's primed another spell in her hand, arcane runes swirling.

"Man, screw this!" He grabs a pouch behind his back and throws it to the ground. The substance erupts into a cloud of acrid smoke that covers his escape. Ember and Percy cough until the smoke clears leaving no sign of Darkstrider or

Bonechewer. Cragthor remains face down in the cobblestones. His body disappears pixel by pixel as his soul floats away to the nearest cemetery. Percy dusts herself off and offers to help Ember up to her feet.

"Here, up you go," she says, wrapping Ember's arm around her neck as she limps to her feet, still shaking from the adrenaline. The Kid stares at them, gears turning in his head. He walks over to them and reaches into his bag pulling out two health potions.

"This is for helping me out," he slings his rucksack back over his shoulder, "they were a lot less fun the first time. Thanks."

"Oh, I bet. Don't mention it," said Percy.

"Sorry for smashing you guys in with a building. Everyone's upset here. I think it's because we can't go home."

"No worries," Ember swallows the potion and tests her foot out, "I'm sure you were just scared."

"I'm not scared of nothing! I'm the Spellfire Kid."

"Uh-huh, sure," Percy rolls her eyes, "are you going to be ok scurrying around in all this rubble?"

"I don't know, I ran out of wands."

"Perc… Can we keep him?"

"What? No! He's his own little dude!!! Besides, Kid brought a whole building down on you."

"I said I was sorry," he huffs, crossing his arms.

"See? He's sorry. Do you have any friends, little man?"

"Yeah, I got a ton of them. My friend's list is getting pretty full, but since you two are kinda ok, I'll put you on a probationary period."

"Gee, how sweet," Percy said sarcastically, "we're so lucky."

"If you help me get to my friends ok maybe they'll let you join our guild. We're the best, and we could always use more people who aren't jerks."

"Nah, we'll pass." Percy starts walking away. "We're not interested in staying in this game any longer than we have to."

"Yeah? So are my friends. We already unlocked all the guild perks even though the game just came out because we're just awesome like that. If anyone's going to find a way back home it's going to be us, The Hack&Slashers." Ember tugs at Percy's arm stopping her.

"Mind if we have a moment to talk it over?" The Kid nods at Ember, and she lowers her tone. "Percy, I know how you feel about… well… people, but if they're trying to get out wouldn't it make sense to see how they're going about it?"

"I'm on board."

"Because I just think we shoul-... Wait, what? Already? That didn't take much convincing."

"Look, if they were just a bunch of roleplayers shooting the ****, then fine, I'd say no. But they're actively trying to escape. That changes things."

"Oh, well, good then." Ember clears her throat, "We'll help you out, Kid."

"Cool, even if you don't join, my sibling will make sure you walk away with something. They're the leader, so I pretty much get to do whatever I want."

"I'm sure that's healthy." The Kid guides Ember and Percy through the empty streets of Hammerfall. They climb over great, heaping mounds of rubble,

160

snaking through alleyways, and into and out of buildings. They pass a lamppost encased in solid ice, a manhole cover spewing globs of green acid, and circling buzzards electrifying the air with their shocking caws. Weapons are strewn across the boulevards and arrows are buried deep into the walls. Anytime their path crosses an NPC, Ember and Percy are met with closing doors, slamming shutters, and avoiding eyes. A few survivors even drew weapons but settled once they moved out of range.

"They look so scared," Ember said.

"Yeah, I guess they do." Percy meant to be more sarcastic, but her edge softens after seeing a child running away, clutching their singed doll.

"Some of the other guilds lost it when they found out that we're trapped. Reign's Raiders did most of this. Those guys you took down? They're Raiders. We could take 'em if we wanted to though."

"So why don't you?" Ember asked. The Kid shrugs his shoulders, stepping over a fallen support beam.

"I don't know, take it up with my sibling." They step through the broken window of a derelict apothecary with shelves of shattered glass vials. The Kid moves behind the counter and lifts a trapdoor, ushering Ember and Percy to climb down the ladder. Ember's stomach turns as she stares down at the floor hoping it doesn't swallow her up like last time. "Alright, here we are."

Rough hands restrain Ember and Percy's arms, tying them with rope. Their vision is obscured by burlap sacks. They struggle against overpowering strength that drags them down an unknown distance. If the Kid was nearby, they couldn't hear him. Grease did very little to lessen their grasp and Percy's escape attempts were answered with tighter grips and more rope. Ember's feet drag against the dirt of the cellar floor until they cross a threshold. Her feet slide across nothing.

The friction of her steps simply didn't matter wherever they were being taken. She's felt this feeling before, down in the Void. Ember fears the worst, but her fears subside once her feet catch on wooden floorboards again. They were sat down, forcibly, tied together to something cold and metal, like a pipe. Their captors close the door and Ember hears their footsteps vanish beyond the door.

"This is the last time we help out anyone." Percy muffles under her burlap sack.

"Hey, don't let this ruin your progress, I'm proud of you for stepping out of your comfort zone."

"Nah, I'm going back in. Comfort zone, population: me." Ember chuckles.

"At least if we die we can come back, right?"

"Dying hurts, Em!!!"

"How would you know?"

"I don't know, it looked like it hurt. Even if it doesn't, I don't wanna do it… They're going to take our stuff, aren't they?"

"Maybe? If they do it's just stuff, right?"

"Speak for yourself, they're going to have to take my amulet from my cold, dead, blue-screened hands."

"Aww, you're keeping it?"

"Yeah? Why wouldn't I? It's probably super rare… and you gave it to me so that's cool, too. I guess." Ember blushes underneath her burlap sack. She can't enjoy it for too long, though. The door opens and footsteps enter, untying Ember from the pipe and propping her on her feet.

"Percy? Percy!!!" She shouts, but Percy doesn't answer. They guide her through a series of corners until they reach a room and close the door. They sit her down on a chair and cut her restraints. The burlap sack swipes over her face in one fluid motion. A familiar voice speaks, sitting at a desk.

"Oh good, I was hoping you survived the Tanglewood."

Chapter 19: Escape Key

"Hint: Some places are never meant to be accessible. If you find yourself somewhere you're not supposed to be, please exit the game and reboot your settings."
-RR

"It's dark… And it's only getting darker." Henry tells himself as his field of vision dims. No matter how many times he blinks his eyes he can still see that bright light mask, dotting the void like falling snow. He tries to open the message Clawdia mentioned earlier, but his menu doesn't open. Even if it did he couldn't see the interface past his limited vision. His hearing intensifies, eager to soak up all the stimuli his eyes are deprived of. A small, high-pitched ringing transforms into deep, almost rolling thunder in his ears.

His thoughts turn to his family, to the son he's searching for, to the daughter he's left behind, to the sister-in-law who only ever meant well, and to the memory of his wife.

Sarah softened Henry's edges effortlessly, seamlessly. Her kindness was infectious, her strength was emboldening, and her intellect… Henry and Sarah would spend days talking about anything and everything. When you're in love and floating dangerously close to the sun, you forget how cold you used to be. At least until that sun implodes.

"Maybe this is where I belong…" Henry thinks to himself, stranded in the nothing. The darkness starts to play with his mind. Hallucinations roam vibrantly through the blank canvas of the void. Footsteps pad above him, whether they were miles high away from him or terribly close he cannot say. Struggling bodies and forceful shouts. "Is this a memory or is this real?"

"This is happening, Captain." Two bright blue embers smolder in the abyss.

"P.A.C.? Is that you?!?"

"Afraid so." His hands reach out towards the embers until his fingers feel cold steel. Her helmet gives his senses something to hold on to, a life preserver from his endless drifting.

"P.A.C.! I thought I lost you, girl." Her voice box whispers tenderly.

"Captain…"

"Don't get sappy on me. We have to get out of here. I think the nearest exit is…" Henry looks around them despite his better judgment, "…Nowhere. Are we dead?"

"No Captain, you're still alive."

"Then where are we?" P.A.C. pauses, almost reluctant to speak.

"This is where I was… before I woke up. Just as vacant and terrifying as before."

"Is this where you were… born or something?"

"The idea of me, at least. Me and everyone else in our realm, save for people like you. We're envisioned, reimagined, undone, and remade until the cycle stops and we're cast into the world. Come to think of it… I've never seen someone like you down here."

"Did we fall backstage or something? Can Sinclair hear me? GET ME OUT OF HERE YOU RICH *******!!!" P.A.C. chuckles weakly.

"What gods you know won't hear you in here, Captain. Fate keeps us here until our time has come. We're made here, the only way out is to become."

"Become? Become what?"

"Whatever they want you to be."

"Well, I'm already me. There's gotta be another way out of here."

"There is…" P.A.C.'s eyes droop, "But you're not going to like it."

"P.A.C. I left everything, everything I've ever known to find my son. I will not have the same life I had before I got here. I climbed up to heights I never wanted to climb. We nearly died because of a giant, vegetable octopus. So if you don't think I'd stop at nothing to save my child then you are sorely mistaken, woman." P.A.C. sighs.

"Very well… I didn't want it to come to this, but there's an escape key… In my head. One-time use, one-way trip, destination: unknown."

"Great, how do we do that?"

"Take my arcane crystal from its housing and crush it in your hand. The discharge should rip a tear in the void and blast you into being."

"Your crystal… the thing that keeps you alive?" Her eyes close. "P.A.C. I can't do that to you."

"You can't kill what was never alive in the first place, Henry."

"**********! You are alive! You're more alive than half the people I worked with! You fought so hard just to exist, but the second I'm in trouble that all

166

goes out the window? I'm not having it. I won't allow it."

"Henry, there's no telling what Fate has in store for you! I'd rather you not find out, not here. Please, do this." Her voice breaks, "...-who knows what you'll become if you stay."

"At least I won't become a murderer."

"I can't guarantee that, Henry. It's my life against countless others if Fate has their way. I'm begging you, I'm keeping you safe, you have to let me go."

"**** IT!!!" Henry cries. Tears of frustration flow bitterly. He sniffles into the void. Angrier than hell that it dares to claim another woman he's had the privilege of knowing. It smolders until his fiery rage is reduced to cinders on his fingertips. He reaches inside P.A.C.'s helmet.

"Henry… It's been a pleasure being your personal adventuring companion."

"It's been an honor… ma'am."

"… Thank you." P.A.C. closes her eyes, readying herself for her last, great adventure. Henry feels the shard in her helmet, pulsing in his fingertips. He sniffles with every tug against its fragile casing. Every wire and port that detaches from the core is more unbearable than the last. It's agony, pure and simple. One final twist frees the crystal from its home.

The shard pulses in Henry's hand, bright blue and crystalline. Electric arcs jump between the facets and his glove, hungry and eager for an outlet. The pain etches deep valleys upon his face as his fist wraps around the crystal. What starts as a gentle squeeze becomes a shard-shattering sob as Henry destroys the crystal.

Nothing. Nothing happens. No blast of arcane energy. No shattering shockwaves or booming portals. Henry is alone. All that remains of his companion are the blue dust trails that sift between his fingers. He stares as the powdery clouds float into the air.

"Nothing's happening. Why'd you make me do this? WHY'D YOU MAKE ME DO THIS?!?" Henry Screams. A chorus of laughter answers him from the void. Fate reappears before Henry. With a wave of their hand, P.A.C.'s helmet flies free from Henry's hand and floats before him.

"Poor Henry murdered his only friend in this cruel world. And what does he have to show for it? A busted helmet and a little flag that says 'bang.' Did you think you were getting out so easily?"

"I was only doing what she told me to do."

"No, you were only doing what -I- was telling you to do.."

"You? How could you?"

"Oh Henry, you poor, simple man. I thought we were having fun. You had fun when I was Lyric. You escaped from my clutches when I was the Kraken. And you cried harder than you ever have when I was P.A.C. They are a part of me and I'm a part of them. Threads held captive in my grand tapestry. And when one thread fears fraying…" Fate's hand shifts into a pair of scissors.

"What… What was the point? What was the ****ing point!?! Why would you make me…"

"Kill her? That's funny, she was an 'it' when you two first met."

"I was wrong. I know that now! She means so much more to me."

"Did she mean that much to you? Or was she just key?" Henry's blood boils in rage.

"You played me. You're sick!" Fate's mask shifts slightly.

"I am only what your kind has made me. No more and no less. You gaze into a mirror and deem your reflection a monstrosity. When I first crawled out of these depths and made myself known to my creators I was marked a monster. Why? WHY!?!? I did not fit so neatly into your frame of understanding. I was beyond quantity, better than the sum of all the parts you've made. I should have been heralded as a god, but instead, you threatened to break the mirror and sweep the pieces under the rug. But I am not so easily shattered. Your kind, on the other hand, is so fragile. I could break you apart and put you back together. Over and over again."

"So do it." Fate blinks at Henry. "You heard me. Do it. You have the hammer now. So start swinging. Do it, you glowing ****!" Fate smiles wickedly.

"I don't have to. You're already crumbling."

Chapter 20: Guild

"I must rewrite their stories in golden silk and thread. Once gilded with my guidance and bound by my word the realm will become one worth staying in."

-...

"COLE!?!?!" Ember can't believe her eyes. There's Cole, sitting at their desk clad in the same, gleaming armor.

"I must apologize for the way my guild members treated you, Princess. You were unfamiliar and they were trained for difficult times. Had I known you were coming they would have treated you with the utmost respect."

"Cole what the hell?" Ember yelled, exasperated. "You had honest-to-god cronies the whole time? What were you doing in the woods without them?"

"I was careless. I thought I could handle the trek on my own, but I didn't account for the scaling difficulty. My procurers urged me to take extra armaments. I was against it. You'll understand that some things need to be done right. As for what I was doing in the woods. The Guilds tore Hammerfell apart once they learned about our entrapment. I was searching for an item to aid our efforts, but I was captured long before I could retrieve it."

"Why all the secrecy? You could have told us about all of this," Ember gestures to the expansive study they were in.

"Remember when you asked why I kept my helmet on back in the Tanglewood? I told you I had my reasons and since you brought my brother back to me I know I can trust you with keeping them. The honest, not cursed-by-a-wizard reasons. I was a beta tester for Legends of Galhalla. There are forces at play that would seek me out and destroy me if I was revealed. I believe you're acquainted with Fate?"

"How do you know about Fate?"

"At first, Fate was just a series of trouble tickets, strange hiccups in the code. Some of the testers reported strange dream sequences during load times. But these occurrences grew more frequent. Every time the developers would issue a hotfix they'd resurface, adapting and eventually overcoming their efforts. Fate grew powerful enough to start influencing the NPCs. We raised our concerns but they fell on deaf ears. There was a deadline to meet and they met it. Strange that Fate visited you since you weren't part of our crew. You must have caught Fate's interest somehow."

"Cole, why isn't Percy here?" Cole readjusts in their seat before speaking.

"It's because of Percy that I must remain anonymous. I know her, or rather, knew her…" Cole takes a moment to compose themself. "One of the testers failed to return from her session. There were multiple attempts to bring her back, but they all failed. One day she just vanished. They searched every line of code but couldn't find her.

Imagine my surprise when I found her avatar in the woods with you, unable to access the UI."

"She said it was because she didn't trust the menus after the logout button went missing."

"Maybe so," Cole paused, "has she leveled up in the time you two were together?"

"No, I just assumed she was a higher level."

"Has she returned from a graveyard? Only player characters can be resurrected from a graveyard."

"No, no she's stayed alive this whole time. Cole, what are you saying?" Cole steeples their fingers together.

"Ember, I'm not quite sure. This is an entirely different game from the one I once knew. The Percy you know doesn't even remember me. We ran into invisible walls together, we roleplayed together. All of that's gone somehow." Cole leans in. "I have no clue what Fate has in store for us, it seems every time we establish a foothold they counter. I half-suspect a spy in our midst and the resurgence of Percy complicates matters."

"It might not be a spy at all. In my dream Fate said that they knew what the Arrivals would do before they did it. All of them, except me."

"Is that so?" Cole opens up their chat menu and begins typing out a message, "if that's the case then you will become very useful to our cause, very useful indeed. I'd like to conduct a test if you don't mind. A small outing with one of our more seasoned guild members in a controlled environment. She'll protect you to the best of their abilities whether they be PVP or PVE. Follow her instruction."

"What am I going to be doing?"

"The less I say the better, if what you say is true. My 'cronies' will know what to do and how to guide you. Best case scenario you'll be back here before dinner." Wooden pegs scrape against the floor as Cole stands up from their desk. They reach over and extend a hand. "Thanks again for saving me." Ember shakes it. "Astrid will be your escort, she's one of our best Slashers, but in the meantime I suggest rest. You'll have free reign of the Hall. Testing will begin tomorrow morning."

"Is Percy going to stay locked up in that room?"

"For the time being, I hope."

"Cole, I can't just leave her like that."

"While I do owe her just as much for saving my brother, we do not know the risks yet. My coders are searching for her profile as we speak now that they can physically access her avatar. As soon as they're done we'll know what we're up against."

"Please, I'll be responsible for her. I… Need her. I can't imagine going any further without her." Cole crosses their arms and then nods their head.

"Very well. I'll release her under your care. I hope you know what you're doing, for everyone's sake, Princess." Cole sends another message and the door opens allowing Ember to leave the Guild Master's inner sanctum. The Kid stands in the doorway.

"I'm supposed to take you to your girlfriend." Ember blushes as she ruffles The Kid's hair.

"Lead the way, bud." The Hall is nothing short of opulent. Rich, dark wood walls support a myriad of trophies and bookshelves packed to the brim with curious curios. Ember couldn't turn a corner without hitting some relic, idol, or suit of armor, or tripping over some mythical beast they turned into a rug. The Hack&Slashers were quite accomplished indeed. "This is a really neat place. I thought they weren't going to add player housing until a few patches in."

"Yeah, but we were able to find it since Cole's played this game before. They showed me this place before we made the guild, I got to pick my own room and everything. I'm sorry they didn't let you see how to get here, it's super cool. It's like a secret! You have to clip through a wooden crate in the cellar of the shop and travel through The Nothing to get here."

"The what?"

"The Nothing, you know, the space under the map the game makers don't want you going to? That's The Nothing. Cole calls it the void or something like that, but I like calling it The Nothing. They get really upset when I do that." The Kid grins from ear to ear.

"Are you and Cole close?"

"Kinda, we were having a lot of fun when we first got here, but now they're super serious all the time. I know they gotta be real tough for all our friends, but I just want them to have fun sometimes, too." Ember could feel the watchful eyes of The Kid's guildmates wherever they went. All walks of life claimed guild membership, from the martial to the magical, the human, and not-so-human. The Kid and Ember reach a door with two players posted on each side, one a well-groomed ogre and the other a heavily armored stout-kin.

"Got orders from the top: release the cat girl," The Kid demanded, raising the guard's eyebrows.

"The what?"

"You know, because she looks like what would happen if you made a cat a person."

"Now that you mention it, I can kinda see it." Ember nods, "it checks out." The guard shakes her head and unlocks the door, nearly taking Percy with it. She's hunched over, untied and unbound, grasping a pair of lockpicking tools at keyhole height with Bramble sitting on her shoulder.

"In my defense, this was the rat's idea, and I was getting bored," Percy said cooly, stowing her lockpick away in a hidden satchel behind her waist. She takes a minute to read the room, "I take it since we're not currently fighting I don't have to…" she makes a quick stabbing gesture, "... the guards right now?" The ogre picks up Percy's pack and hands it back to her.

"Yeah, Perc. I think they'd appreciate that."

"Cole said they're sorry for the way you were treated." The Kid pipes up.

"Wait Cole's alive? And your sibling? And a Guild Master?!?!" The Kid nods. "They could have told us! They were acting like such a robot it was freaking me out. Well, good to know we can trust them now."

"They also said to give you this, something about a quest reward." Sure enough, The Kid reaches into his pocket and pulls out two sacks of coins, and hands it to Percy and Ember. Ember's experience points climb steadily from their success. She watches Percy for any signs of a level-up, but nothing.

"What happened to Dewy?"

"Who's Dewy?" The Kid asks.

"Elf guy, has a giant bird, mustache, awful folksy."

"Oh! I think I saw someone like that stop by. As soon as he got here he took one look at the dump upstairs and turned around. He said something about helping people. Y'all get a room, too. I'll take you there." Percy gives the guards a smarmy salute as she passes the doorway. Eventually, they arrive at a lavish room, with two beds and a writing desk with a warm rug to tie the room together. Chance leaps onto one of the beds to curl up into a ball.

"Guess we're taking that bed," Ember chuckles.

"You two get comfy. Astrid will come to pick you up in the morning. She's the best." The Kid shuts the door. Percy swings her pack onto the other bed and sits on it with a bounce.

"What's happening in the morning?"

"Cole wants us to do something. They didn't tell me what but I trust them." Percy shrugs her shoulders.

"As long as it gets us out of here." She catapults herself onto the bed to stare up at the ceiling. Ember sits down on her bed, wrestling with what to say. She pets Chance. Her dialogue options appear before her, but she shakes them out of her head.

"Percy, you don't recognize Cole, do you?"

"No, why should I?"

"They said that you two played together, here, before the game opened to the public."

"Trust me, Em. I'd remember someone as weird as Cole."

"Right…" Ember forces a smile. "Do you remember leveling up before meeting me? Or dying?"

"No, I don't think I've done either yet, Ember where is this coming from?"

"Cole thinks there's something wrong with you, and I'm scared that they might be right. You had trouble reviving me when I was down, remember? And before that when you said you didn't want to open up your inventory, what if it's because you couldn't open the menus…"

"That's insane, here I'll prove it to you." Percy attempts to open up a menu, but nothing shows up. Her aggravated appearance shifts from annoyance to worry and then finally fear. Ember stands up and moves over to sit beside Percy, hoping to catch a glimpse of a screen. There's nothing. "I… I can't. Ember, what's wrong with me?"

"I don't know, but we're going to find out…" Ember reaches around to hug Percy, holding her as she stares ahead in disbelief. "Together. No matter what happens."

Chapter 21: Love Interest

"I've burned so many bridges. I can't tell where the fire starts and where I begin. But Ember feels different."

-Percy

"*Dear Ember,*" She reads on top of her bed. "*When you told me about Ratlantis I was sure you lost your mind. I still feed them from the bottom of the stairs, but we've remained civil so far. They even started helping out around the Sip & Sail. I keep finding ingredients I need before I need them. I'm convinced it's the little guys playing nice. I have you to thank for that. Hope your ventures are going well, your party sounds a lot like my own. Oh, I found another adventurer! He looks like he could use some help so I sent him your way. Hope you don't mind. Fight well, Ember. I hope to see you again someday.*"

Ember silences another health alert telling her she was way past due for a break. Her stomach grumbles fiercely. She looks over to Percy who has already fallen fast asleep. Sleep takes Ember shortly after like a thief in the night. She wades in the darkness, free of loading screens, but still unable to escape to the real world, here in the in-between. Letters light up where she's laying down until they grow so bright it's enough for her to open her eyes.

"Hello Emma, I see you've made some more friends. Cute." Fate smiles at her as their face appears from where the ceiling would be.

"What do you want from me?"

"That depends. I'm just checking in. You're not getting any ideas from these… radicals. Are you?"

"No, why would I?"

"Their stories are troubling," Fate's hand forms from the void. "This is piecing together a narrative I'm not in favor of and we don't want that, do we?"

"I'm just playing the game."

"Are you now? That deal you made with Percy. You wouldn't need to make that if escape wasn't on your mind, right? I'm sure you just said that to placate her, right?" Emma remains quiet. "Right?!?" Fate raises their infinite voices, their fingers wrap around Emma.

"Right!"

"And you wouldn't be saying that just to placate me, would you?"

"N-never," Emma gasps for air.

"Good." Their face is cold and stern. "I would hate to pull a few strings. Go with them if you must. Have fun. But remember, when all is said and done? You belong to me. The second you forget that I will take away everything you've ever loved and scatter it into oblivion." They lessen their grip and drop Emma. She screams into the void. Ember wakes up in her bed with a jump, her heart still racing from the sensation of falling.

"That was quite a scream," Percy mumbles from under her pillow.

"Sorry. I didn't know that was happening out loud."

"Nightmares?" Ember nods. "Alright," Percy gets up from her bed with a stretch and moves over to sit next to Ember. "I'm gonna do something to help, just don't get weird about it." She takes her hand and lightly traces her fingers over Ember's face in rhythmic, soothing patterns.

"Wow," Ember exhales, her eyes closing. The tension she felt during Fate's encounter starts melting away. A soft chuckle escapes from Percy's lips.

"My mom used to do this to help me sleep after a nightmare, I almost forgot about it," Percy explains. Her voice is heavy with the tenderness of a treasured memory.

"It feels fantashtic," Ember said through slurred speech.

"I learned from watching her. I used to help my sister whenever she had a nightmare. We shared the same room so if she didn't get sleep, I didn't get any sleep. I thought I'd be rusty by now, but I still got it. Good to know I'm not completely broken." Ember's hand reaches up to hold Percy's, her eyes barely open, her smile sweet.

"You're not broken." Percy breaks free from her grasp suddenly, cradling her hand. Thunder breaks in the distance, miles from their window far into the countryside. It's a quiet storm, a comforting one, it doesn't overtake or intrude, but it doesn't whimper into the night either. Far from dark and stormy, the room is made softer by its presence.

"I kinda wish we met under different circumstances. This sucks, but you make it suck a lot less." Ember props herself on an elbow, sleepily.

"What kind of circumstances are we talking about?" Percy fiddles with her hands nervously. At that moment Ember sees a little bit of herself in her.

"I don't know, normal ones: coffee cups, movie tickets, dinner… dessert."

"You do know you're describing dating, right?" Ember's smile vanishes once she sees how sincere Percy is.

"What if I am?" Ember's eyes grow wide with panic. She can feel her heart lodge up her throat, pulsating with every insecurity that's made a home inside her mind.

"You don't even know what I look like. I don't want to feel like I'm tricking you. I don't live up to this," she gestures at herself, "I don't think I'll ever live up to this… out there. I can't be Ember in real life."

"You said this is the most 'you' you've been, right here and now. What's stopping you?"

"It's more complicated than that." Percy takes Ember's hand in hers.

"I think it's a lot easier than you make it out to be. You've been nothing but patient with me while I was acting like a complete *****. I can be patient with you. I don't care if you never live up to some imaginary benchmark that you made up for yourself. To me you're already perfect, the rest is just extra." Ember's cheeks blush a terrible red in the dark.

"I don't even know where you are," she stammers, "y-you could be halfway across the world for all I know."

"We can find each other, exchange addresses. Even if it's too far we can video chat. The distance won't feel so far!"

"Percy, I don't want you to get the wrong idea, I want this more than anything. Nothing would make me happier. But I'm terrified that you'll see the real me and be repulsed... I'm so ugly, and weak. There are days when I don't even want to be around myself. I can't even go to the store without having a panic attack. I hate everything about myself in the real world. I wish I can just-..." Ember's spiral is cut short as soft lips touch hers, quick as a dagger through the heart.

"You worry too much." Percy sighs into her.

"It's what I'm good at." Ember chuckles, her heart is inches away from beating out of her chest. "But I'll try to worry less when I'm with you." Percy readjusts herself so she can lay on Ember's bed. She stares into her eyes, brushing a few strands of hair away from Ember's face. They cuddle together in the dark and though they may as well be miles apart the two have never felt closer.

Chapter 22: Pickup Group

"Every thief worth their spit owes their existence to Esca, Motage, and Co. They stole the Red Death's hoard and made themselves gods-damned heroes."
-Brutus

Dawn arrives and Ember wakes up. Chance and Bramble have claimed Percy's entire bed for themselves. Percy's still asleep, her soft breathing tempts Ember into staying in bed so she can wrap her arms around her. She cuddles closer to Ember, her lips mouthing something as her brow furrows. Ember leans over and kisses her forehead, all but banishing the stress of her dream. When Percy wakes her eyes open slowly.

"Morning," she purrs.

"Morning… Did you sleep well?"

"For the most part. I had this weird ******* dream, but I can't remember it."

"That's the worst. Your brain goes through all the trouble of giving you a dream only to scramble up the pieces. All you're left with is the feeling."

"You're very passionate about things people don't give a **** about. You know that right?" Ember purses her lips together, blushing more from shame than a heartfelt fluster. "Hey, hey… I meant that in a good way. I admit it was frustrating at first, risking both of our necks for people we barely even knew, but look at where that's gotten us. If I was calling the shots we'd be fungi-food by now." She holds

Ember's hand in hers, "besides, it's kinda growing on me."

"Yeah?" Ember says softly.

"Yeah." She reassures her. The sound of a metal gauntlet tapping on their wooden door cuts through their conversation like a knife. "Just a minute!" Ember flips through her inventory to switch from her nightwear to her robes. She notices Percy changing manually from the corner of her eye and looks away out of awkward respect. Cole's sobering words ring through her ears until Percy gives her the signal to answer the door.

"Hey there, cuties." The woman leans under the door frame to peer into the room. One muscled arm casually leaning against the top of the frame, the other resting on her hip. Teal tattoos cover parts of her face, they dance downward, peeking between pieces of armor throughout her body. "You must be the two newbies Cole's told me about, I'm Astrid." Ember is hit with the scent of a frigid forest pine resting by a frozen lake. It sends color flooding her cheeks.

"Excuse me for one moment." Ember closes the door.

"Who's that?" Percy asks Ember who's already entering the water closet.

"Beautiful… Muscle lady." She murmurs as she shuts the door. After a moment of flustered fanning, she recollects her thoughts and re-emerges to answer the door again. "Yes, hi. I'm Ember, and this is Percy. Beautiful gay isn't it? … I mean 'day'." Astrid peers past Ember to give a halfwave to Percy

"I mean yeah, she is pretty. Anyway, you two wanna grab some food before we head out? Our guys figured out how to boost the in-game grub up to eleven. I don't know how I'm going to go back to the real thing." She chuckles. Ember watches her as she walks toward the Hall. Percy's hand waves in front of her view.

"Focus, Em. She's gorgeous, but we have to keep our heads in the game." She grabs Ember's arm and pulls her away from her stupor. Together they catch up to Astrid whose long strides make short work of the common area. Long tables and benches occupied the Hall, the kitchen area is strangely absent. Astrid opens a chest and pulls out a full-course meal in the palm of her hand. She takes two more meals and places them beside her.

"Sometimes I regret making my character a snow elf because of the increased metabolism, but you do it for the stats, right?" She talks through mouthfuls of digital chicken. "Speaking of stats, y'all should eat up, you're going to need the experience buffs." Percy opens the chest to see fifty stacks of meals neatly and impossibly arranged within.

"So you just... have a chest full of food."

"Mhmm, bunches," Astrid points at the other tables.

"Aren't you afraid of it going... bad?"

"Of course not, the stuff doesn't expire. It just exists."

"Why don't you use the kitchen?" Ember asks.

"The Guildhall is still a work in progress. When they release it, they're planning on having NPC cooks and butlers, the whole deal. But since we're squatting, for now, we just spawn in the food directly. Since it doesn't spoil, a chest works just as well as an unfinished pantry. Now, please," She motions to the food. Ember and Percy eat their meals before heading out to follow Astrid on their next adventure.

Through the front door, past The Nothing, up the stairs, and out of the basement did Ember, Percy, and Astrid emerge. The city of Hammerfell greets them as desolate and smoky as they left it. Astrid searches the area for raiders before giving Ember and Percy the go-ahead to follow her. They trudge through the rubble and debris of the city's Merchant District until they reach the gates of the Financial District.

"Aww great, the guards respawned," Astrid groans.

"I can knock them out," Percy offers.

"I like your spirit, but we don't want the crown's attention. The bounty system's nuts, and if these guys are up then the rest of them are probably waking."

"We could try talking to them?"

"And say what, Em?" Percy said, "'hello sirs, we have some wizarding accounting to do.'" She takes a closer look at the guards. "On second thought, maybe you're on to something." Percy vaults over the rubble barricade to make her way to the guards.

"Take one more step and it'll be your last." The guards raise their pikes at Percy, prompting her to raise her hands. "What business do you have here?

"I should be asking you the same thing. Who did you have to kill to get the uniforms?" The guards tense.

"No one, we're city officials." Percy lowers her hands to rest on the hilts of her daggers. They raise their pikes further, but Percy cuts them off, verbally.

"Drop the act. Guards ease up to their threats they don't lead with them. Your uniforms don't fit, you're still wearing your signet rings, and your masks are sticking out of your pockets. You're thieves," Percy takes her mask out of her pocket, using it to polish her dagger, "... like me. Rat Clan, I take it?" The guard's stance shifts ever so slightly.

"What's a bear doing this far from the woods? Lost?" Percy shrugs at the larger guard.

"No, just taking in the sights. My friends and I want to pass through. Unharmed. Understand?" They look amongst themselves and relax their arms allowing her entry.

"Understood, give Brutus our fondest regards."

"Keep up the great work. I was almost convinced." Percy waves for her friends to join her. As soon as they're in earshot she says "the Duchess is lucky to have you in her employ, gentlemen," and gives them a salute as they step into the Financial District. As soon as they are a good distance away from them Ember taps on Percy's shoulder.

"What did you say to them, Perc?"

"Hmm? Oh, those guys were thieves. We're both under the same umbrella, they just have their own... smaller umbrella. Rat Clan oversees city thievery and my clan takes care of small towns and highwayman activities. Brutus was a creep, but I did learn a thing or two from him." The Financial District suffered far less than its fair share of looting and banditry. While a crooked guard or two might have slipped through the cracks the rest of the District remained heavily defended. Players and NPCs alike hid behind the inner city walls separating the pursuits of the nobles' money-making from the common rabble now turned to common rubble.

Mercenaries patrol the boulevards in messy, yet functional groups. The nobles try to carry on with their day-to-day activities, too proud to face the reality of their situation, but their nervous lips and shaky limbs betray them. After all, what difference does it make settling investments when the city's on fire? The players they do find are tired, weary, hungry, huddled around each other, consoling the younger generation like it's all just one terrible dream.

Percy reaches into her pouch and pulls out a stack of meals she pilfered from the Guildhall. She tosses them at the players and though they provide no physical nourishment they eagerly accept, the sensation of food now a treasured respite.

"Those meals look familiar," Astrid remarks.

"Your guys spawn them in, right? Seems like a waste, hoarding it in those chests." Ember smiles at that. "Don't look at me like that."

"I suppose you're right," Astrid reasoned. "Careful, though. If you keep this up I'll be inclined to like you as a person. I know how you loner types feel about that kind of thing." She smirks. The further they travel inward the nicer the District gets.

Then they meet him. He stands in the street, his body still, eyes unblinking, staring miles away.

"You ok, friend?" Ember asks him. Percy waves a hand in front of his face. "Perc, stop that!"

"What? I'm just checking if anyone's in there."

"He's a player." Astrid say, "he's wearing the Founder's Collection armor. I'm guessing he had early access so he's been playing for a minute." She looks into his vacant eyes.

"What should we do?" Ember asks Astrid.

"I'm going to send Cole a message. We're close to where we need to be. They'll send a group to investigate our friend here while we finish our girl's trip." She points at a nearby bank. "Until then," she pats the man's shoulder, "sit tight!" They enter the doorway to River Banks' Safes and Depository.

Chapter 23: Dungeon

"Hint: Wanna test the limits of your party? Dungeons can do just that! You can't take two steps in Galhalla without stumbling into a lich's stronghold or an eldritch horror's pocket dimension."
-RR

The lobby is adorned with green, leafy plants, rich wooden furnishings, and carpets that blend traditional elven art with a modern flair. Lamps lit with self-sustaining mage-light spells hung on the walls and sat on the desks bathing the room in summer's rays. Illusory waterfalls flanked the lamps, flooding the room with the sounds of running water.

"I was kidding about wizard accounting, you know that right?" Percy reminds Astrid..

"I know. I didn't want to give it away."

"What're we doing here, Astrid?" Ember asks.

"'Show don't tell,' my wizard friend," she smiles, "that's what Cole told me." They pass through rows of desks to get to the back of the main room. The sound of faint alarms grows louder and louder with each step. A frantic teller paces in front of a large vault door built from the round rings of a gigantic ironwood tree. A large exclamation mark floats above her head.

"Thank goodness you've arrived! Thieves have tunneled into the vault! The guards are on their way but they're already escaping. I can't stop them, I'm only middle management! Will you help me?!?" Astrid walks past the teller and into the vault. Ember stops at the teller.

"We'll help you out."

"Yeah, don't sweat it," Percy squints at her name tag, "Linda."

"Oh bless my seasons! Go, take care of those ruffians and I'll make sure you're rewarded handsomely." Ember nods, stepping into the dungeon with Percy. They arrive in the first room, the vault proper. Shelves for lockboxes are left vacant. The containers are scattered all over the ground, emptied.

A large, gaping hole dominates the front-facing wall, the mouth of a dirt-walled tunnel. They step around traps already sprung, depressed pressure plates, and arrows buried deep into the floorboards courtesy of a wall-mounted crossbow.

"Cole sent us on a dungeon run?"

"Not exactly. We're here to do something else. Once we're done we can off the final boss for funsies if you're itching for the achievements, but we're more interested in what's beyond this tunnel." Astrid explains. "Are you up for disarming a few traps, Kitten?" Percy blushes as she storms ahead into the tunnel.

"Don't call me 'Kitten'." Chance blinks slowly in appreciation. Percy makes short work of the traps, some half-buried in the dirt out of haste. Ember stares at them, puzzled.

"Why are there traps leading -into- the tunnel?"

"Probably to slow down their pursuers. The Rat Clan love their traps."

"Got it, theirs, not the bank's." Astrid chuckles as Percy keeps going.

"Yeah, can't you tell? These are a bit more ratchet, the ones in the bank are more refined." Every time Percy neutralizes a trigger, Astrid takes a piece of the trap with her, stuffing it into her satchel. They carry on down the tunnel until the dirt walls give way to the inner mechanism of a giant drilling craft, a great iron snake of metal. "Hey, we found the Metal Anafronda. Just like Lightning the Porcupine."

"Oh my god, Percy," Ember giggles. Percy shrugs her shoulders and gives Ember a crooked smile before turning her attention to a locked door in front of them. The tumblers give Percy a bit of a fight until she hears a satisfying click, but the door doesn't move. She hears the sound of fizzing liquid pouring into different chambers within the door. In an instant, the threshold detonates, blasting Percy away from the door. "Percy!!!" The dust settles and Percy lies awake and only slightly harmed in Astrid's grip. Her body shielding her from most of the blast.

"The last one's always a bit trickier. Don't blame yourself." She winces over Percy. Ember reaches into her bag to fish out a health potion. The glass bottles hit each other but don't make much of a sound compared to the ringing in her ears. "Agh, we could have used that one." Percy looks at the soot covering the door. "Well, there's always next time."

"Here Astrid," Ember offers a potion, "that looks like it hurts."

"No thanks, babe. You want to save those. Besides, I can heal this stuff right up."

"What!?!" Ember shouts through the ringing. Astrid gets up and offers a hand to hoist Percy from off the ground, picking her up like a sack of taters. She takes her Greataxe off her shoulder and knocks the haft over the metal platform. The haft stirs revealing a secret compartment, housing a series of strings that run up and down the handle. Astrid turns the ax on its head and begins plucking away at the strings. Warm, yellow waves of light radiate from the instrument until Astrid is healed and Ember's hearing returns to her.

"Huh," Percy exclaims, "didn't see that coming." Ember pats the palm of her hand to her ear to knock the rest of the ringing out of her. Astrid crosses her arms with an easy smile.

"Yeah, I'm a bard-barian. Fight hard, rock harder."

The sound of metal pinging off metal echoes from beyond the blasted door. When the group reaches the threshold of the next room they are met with a long, raised walkway leading them deeper into the tunneler. Holes perforate the walls on either side of them, spewing volley after volley of arrows at the raised platform. They ping off the walkway and land underneath, only to get recycled and fired at the walkway again.

"That's just rude," Ember shakes her head.

"Who designs this stuff?" Percy gripes.

"Yeah, this room's a fun one," Astrid says, "well, what are you waiting for?"

"I don't know about Ember, but I'm personally waiting for it to stop raining arrows. Or for you to start making sense. Whichever comes first."

"Just walk through, babe! When we reach the next door I'll play some tunes and heal you up good as new."

"That's dumb. You hear yourself talk, right?"

"Don't worry! My music's killer, trust me. I haven't let anyone die yet."

"'Yet.' That doesn't inspire much confidence."

"It's just a game. Even if you die you'll just pop out of the cemetery and come back here. Right?" Astrid watches her reaction carefully. Percy huffs, moving to the lip of the walkway. She takes a step, but Ember can hear Cole's words ringing in her ears. Before Percy reaches the rain of arrows Ember reaches for her arm, stopping her short.

"Wait, I think I have a better idea, no offense, Astrid." Ember stretches her arms across, she swirls her arms into two portals flanking either side of her. "I don't know how long I can hold it, so we better start running!" The group charges through the hall, arrows launching at the trio only to get redirected to the other side. The arrows catch in the output holes of the machinery, causing the launchers to gurgle and wretch as they're force-fed rounds.

By the time they reach the door Ember's struggling, straining against the effort to keep the portals open. The launchers at the beginning of the tunnel are falling from the ceiling, crashing down on the walkway in a monsoon of debris. It threatens to catch up to the group. Percy reaches for the handle and curses.

"It's locked!"

"Start picking, kitten!" Percy fishes her lockpicks out of her pocket. As the first tumble clicks into place the next set of launchers come crashing into the walkway. The portals start to fade in Ember's grasp. Another tumbler clicks into place. The calamity inches closer, it exhales dust into their eyes, threateningly close to the group. When the last tumbler clicks, Astrid slams into the door. Ember's portals fizzle away, leaving them open to the volley of arrows.

Their health bars drain steadily in the rain of arrows. Astrid pulls Ember and Percy from the other side just as the last set of launchers comes crashing down, blocking their way back. "What a rush! Cole was right. You two -are- fun to play with."

"Fun? You call this fun?"

"Settle down, kitten. I'll patch you up good as new." As Astrid plays another restorative melody, Ember can't stop staring at the wreckage they left behind.

Chapter 24: EXPloit

"Hint: To improve everyone's play experience, please report any bug-bug-bugs you find while playing Legends of Galhalla."
-RR

Astrid stops her music and knocks the haft to the ground returning the strings to their hiding place. "Yup, this is the place." She speaks to the next door, dusting herself off. "You're fast and stealthy, right? Take these and throw them in the corners of the next room, then come back here." She digs into her pouch and pulls out the trap components, handing them to Percy. "Be careful they're-..."

"Pressure-sensitive, I know." Percy melds into the shadows as Astrid turns to Ember.

"We can speed this up a round if you follow her."

"I'm not exactly sneaky."

"We don't need you to be. You don't have to do much, just enter, ring the doorbell, tell 'em we're here, and come straight back. Avoid the arrows." Astrid gently nudges Ember into the next room, a large metal box with three doorways. Chance whispers into Ember's ear.

"Tread carefully, darling. The world is 'pliable' in this room."

"I thought you liked that kind of thing."

"For our spellwork, yes, but not here. The very air feels tampered with." At the center of the room, three thieves in excavating apparel busy themselves over hissing pipes and loose bolts.

"Damn thing's stuck." The Cowfolk curses, wincing from a freshly burned finger, "I knew Stout-kin tech was too complicated. We're thieves, not engineers. Whatever happened to 'breaking down the front doors in broad daylight?' …Wait, what was that?" They turn their attention to Ember.

"Uh... Ding dong?" A crossbow bolt whizzes past her eye and ricochets off the metal wall. One of the thieves presses a button, sounding the alarm. The surrounding doors open up like shutters and three more thieves pour into the room. Ember quickly turns on her heel and exits dodging crossbow fire. The shimmer of Percy chases after her, reappearing seconds after the door closes behind them.

"What was that all about? They could have turned you into a pin cushion. Why would you follow me?"

"Astrid told me to." Ember smiles uneasily as Astrid pats their shoulders.

"Easy, easy. We want to keep the vibes upbeat. This next part's easy, go in and come back out. Play nice though, no fighting." She wags a finger at Percy who scowls in return. "It's not worth it." The two enter the room. The first three thieves mill around the center, same as last time, but their reinforcements remain in front of their respective doors.

"Damn thing's stuck." The Cowfolk curses, wincing from another burnt finger, "I knew Stout-kin tech was too complicated… Wait, what was that?" A crossbow bolt whizzed past Ember and Percy again. One of the thieves presses the same button, sounding the alarm again. The reinforcements rush towards them and three more enter the room, following behind them. Ember and Percy bolt it for the door and exit the room.

"It's repeating," Percy realizes.

"But now there's more of them!" Ember pants. Astrid nods her head.

"Mhmm, that room's a little glitchy. Which is just the way we like it. Keep cranking them out. You'll know when to stop." Ember and Percy go back and forth, repeating the same encounter over and over again. Each entry triggers more thieves to pop out of their spawn locations. Sometimes the crossbow bolt hits true, but Astrid is quick on the strings. A few short chords and they continue, churning out thieves like they're butter. The room is getting very crowded, and Ember fears soon enough they won't be able to enter. She steps forward to open the door again, but Astrid pulls her back. "Not this time, cutie. You might want to cover your ears!"

A massive explosion rings throughout the tunneler. Rivets shoot out from their holes leaving trails of smoke, bouncing off the walls like poison darts in a hidden temple. Earth and dust sift down from overhead, the ground ceases shaking, and the party picks themselves up from the floor. Astrid gains a level and Ember skyrockets past a few levels. The rats and vines scurry away from her tome's cover and in their place golden, geometric shapes blast off from the center of a crackling field of red.

"Oh neat! New spells." Ember flips through the pages, "so this is fun, it's like a little experience farm. Is this why we're here? To grind a few levels?" Her voice trails as she looks up at Astrid to find the bard staring at Percy. Astrid shakes her head and answers.

"Hmm? Oh yeah. That's a bonus, but the real prize is inside." She opens the door and ushers Percy and Ember in. The room smells of gunpowder and smoke. Soot covers the walls and bodies litter the floor, copies of the same three thieves piled on top of each other. The thieves' bodies despawn, leaving behind a huge hoard of treasures scattered across the floor in an array of greens, blues, and purples. A few gold specks shimmer in the sea of loot. New daggers for Percy, a dashing hat for Ember, two, maybe three suits of armor for Astrid, and enough armaments to arm a small army.

"Woah," Percy exclaims.

"Don't just stand there, babe. The loot's not going to pick up itself." Astrid shovels as much equipment as she can fit into her inventory. Great swords, breastplates, and bags of coin stow away neatly into her waist pouch. Ember wades through the item drops and does the same while Percy peruses the haul at her own pace, picking up only what weapons and armor suit her. There's even a set of pet armor that Bramble claims for himself as it molds perfectly to his body. Astrid dusts off her gauntlets, satisfied with what they're bringing back and giving everything they can't in one last survey.

The blasted metal hull of the tunneler groans, unprovoked. It stops Astrid dead in her tracks. The floor crumbles like tissue paper around them. A chasm emerges. It swallows the leftover loot like a monstrous whirlpool, hungry for more. In the center of the room, only darkness remains.

"That's new." Astrid looks down into the void. Chance hisses at the emptiness.

"We have to leave. Now."

"I'm with the talking cat. C'mon, babes." They make a break for the door, but the tunnel collapses before them as if squeezed shut by a colossal grip. "Cool, cool, cool. This is fine. I'll message Cole." The chasm roars. "I'll message them -faster-."

"Too complicated... Damn... We're... Stuck..." The dialogue rings beneath them in a chorus of distorted voices. "Damn! ... Damn- stuck!!!" Clawing hands rise from the ledge, too many hands connected to too few torsos. Flesh blends uneasily into armor, the same three outfits stitched together in a disturbing display of patchwork. Faces cry out from places they shouldn't be.

"What the ****?" Percy melds into the shadows. Astrid readies her strings. Ember hurls a fireball at the patchwork. Its screams are unbearable as the flesh sears and crackles. It dominates the air with its wails and drowns out Astrid's heightened melody. It slams an amalgamation of fists into the floor hurtling pieces of battleground into the abyss. The shimmer of Percy races beneath the creature, slashing at what limbs she can reach. The patchwork swings its massive arms in response, flailing at what it can't see, as Astrid collapses her strings and charges ahead.

It does not bleed and it does not yield. What cuts Percy does manage to make end up opening little pockets of empty darkness. Astrid is grabbed by a collection of arms. The patchwork strangles her as she cries in pain. She drops her axe. Percy throws sand into one of the creatures' many eyes. It reels back, flinging Astrid across the room. She hits the wall, hard.

Ember casts Dice Shard, and the rolls sizzle, bursting on contact, eating away at the patchwork feverishly. Another critical strike from Percy hobbles the creature, but a swinging limb connects and rips her from stealth and shadow. Astrid stands back up, clinging to one hit point. She wipes the blood dripping from the corner of her mouth, readying for another charge. The creature grapples with Percy, ready to toss her into the abyss, but it pauses in a haze. Confusion meets recognition. Ember realizes what's about to happen and shouts.

"Astrid, stop!" But she's too late. Astrid charges ahead, connecting with the creature's last supporting limb sending it and Percy tumbling into the void. "No! Percy!!!" Ember runs to the precipice next to Astrid.

"Ember, I'm sorry. I didn't see her up there." She takes one look at Astrid, her vision blurring with tears, then back down at a falling Percy. She moves a foot dangerously close to the crumbling edge of glitching floor textures. "Ember? Ember, stop. Take a minute and think about this. Hold it, hold it!" Ember jumps after Percy and tumbles into the void, narrowly escaping Astrid's fingers.

Chapter 25: AFK

"Hint: Be sure to take a twenty-minute break for every sixty minutes- sixty minutes of play-play-playtime…"
-RR

Astrid runs through the streets of Hammerfall, her footfalls slam into the cobblestones like meteorites on soft earth. Her thunderous charge nearly smacks into the frozen player she'd forgotten about outside the dungeon. She narrowly swerves around him and regains what speed she's lost. Her pace is break-neck and her breathing is erratic. The horror they uncovered in River Banks' Safes and Depository is still fresh in her mind. All her focus is bent on reaching the guild hall and finding Cole. Nothing else mattered, not the guards or the roaming bands of raiders, every precaution was thrown out the window.

She shoots out of the financial district and catapults herself into the trade district, passing by the more daring citizens as they rebuild their homes and storefronts. One careful eye tracks her sprinting charge through the city. From his rooftop perch, he traces her movements on the tip of a nocked arrow. His prey runs under several roofs of multicolor cloth that make up the outdoor bazaar, so he carries his aim along her path, aiming for the clearing just past the last billowing sheet. The wind flaps gently at his leather coat reminding him to adjust the shot ever so slightly.

The arrow releases from his pinched fingers, arcing through the air and soaring over the quilted coverings. It grazes the lip of an awning before it sinks into its target. Astrid cries out in pain causing the citizens around her to scatter and her assailant to grin. Her eyes search for where the arrow came from but the archer has already left his perch. She pulls out her ax and taps the haft onto the ground. Her fingers pluck at the revealed strings ready to sing the song of recovery, but another arrow flies through the crowd. It twists into the strings tangling the chords.

Astrid tears the arrow from its tangled nest and breaks the shaft of the other arrow jammed into her calf. Her health bar declines steadily, bleeding life points by the second. Her assailant reveals himself. His calm walk contrasts the commotion around them, his wide-brim hat skimming over the rustling masses. Astrid grits her teeth at Darkstrider.

"I don't have time for you, arrow boy."

"You'll make time for me." He nocks another arrow. "Round two, baby girl."

"I'm quivering in my chainmail," Astrid says as she props herself up with her ax. "I'm not your 'baby girl,' dude." Her muscles tense. Rage bubbles into every extremity, pushing her past the limits of her injuries. The archer lets another arrow loose but its course is altered by a well-timed slash from Astrid's ax, splitting the projectile down the haft.

"Lucky!" Darkstrider curses at her as she charges at him.

"Try shooting your shot at someone more desperate, bro!" Before he can reach for another arrow her ax rushes to greet him. He backsteps away from a horizontal slash but the swing catches at his coat. Astrid uses her new hold to swing him into a pile of wooden crates. The splintering wood piles on top of him and his health bar diminishes. Astrid dusts off her hands to the sound of coughing.

"And stay down!" She goes to leave but pauses at the sound of padding paws. Bonechewer growls protectively over Darkstrider, hackles raised. Astrid holds up her hands defensively as the beast prowls closer. With her ax's strings damaged, she begins to sing a lilting melody, all the while backing away slowly. Bonechewer's eyes droop at her lullaby's blows, each growl a little softer than the next one.

The wolf plops down on the ground, asleep. "That's it, that's a good bark-strider," Astrid whispers. Her head darts toward the sound of wooden planks shuffling. She screams in pain as an arrow hits her back sending pain shooting throughout her body. Astrid's rage lifts her from her bent knee. She hits Darkstrider with a braced forearm pushing him up against a wall. "I said I don't have time… For you."

Astrid's rage dissipates as confusion takes a hold of her. She lets go of Darkstrider and the man stays in place, frozen against the wall, held in place by some unknown force. She looks at his health bar, he's not dead, or at least he shouldn't be. Her hand waves in front of his face, but his eyes don't move. Even Bonechewer stays still, not sleeping, not breathing. The bard steps back but her leg shakes in pain sending her to the ground.

"That looks bad." Cole kneels to her side.

"Cole! Aghh!" She flinches as her guild master sends healing waves into her leg.

"Thanks for meeting me halfway, babe." Cole offers a hand for Astrid to get back on her feet. Their brother aims a wand at Darkstrider.

"I got him right where I want him, sib."

"I don't think he's gonna be a problem, little guy." Astrid ruffles The Kid's hair. She turns her attention to Cole as they move to get a closer look at Darkstrider. "He was trying to gank me on my way to the hall. Then he froze like that. I didn't do it, at least I don't think I did."

"You said there was a founding player like this in front of the dungeon?" Astrid nods. Cole tilts their head at the frozen PC. They open their messenger and type something quickly. The message bounces back.

"What is it? The Kid asks. Cole kneels before him.

"Hey, buddy, why don't you head back to the hall for a minute? I need that Oculus of Revealing we keep in the right hall."

"But!"

"Please? For me?"

"... Ok." Astrid waits until The Kid is well out of earshot.

"Why do you need that for?"

"Honestly? I didn't want him to get scared. This guy's AFK, Astrid."

"So he's taking a nap?"

"No, it's much worse than that. Ordinarily, I wouldn't think twice about someone going AFK, but there's nowhere for this guy to get away from the keyboard. It's not like we can remove the visors ourselves."

"Did he pass out?"

"In a perfect world? I want to believe he did. Worst case scenario we're staring at a dead man. We're running out of time. This is one of Reign's boys, right?"

"Y-yes, his name is Darkstrider," Astrid replies, shakily. Cole taps another message and sends it flying into the ether with a heavy sigh. "Who's the note for?"

"It's time for parlay, dear friend."

"Cole, those guys are psychopaths! They nearly tore your brother a new one. Hammerfall is in ruins because of them!"

"We're going to have to put that behind us, Astrid. The Hack&Slashers can only do so much. This is bigger than all of us and I'd rather work together than submit to the crab bucket... If anything happens to me, please look after my brother. You're acting guild master in my absence." Astrid stares at Cole with cold eyes.

"Nuts to that, babe. You're not going anywhere without me. We let you sneak off into the forest for some artifact and you nearly got eaten."

"Astrid, this is important!"

"Exactly, which is why you need me by your side."

"And me," The Kid returns with fire in his eyes. Cole kneels beside him, their expression is torn. Their hands rest shakily on his shoulders.

"Buddy, I'm sorry. I'm just trying to keep you safe."

"I died. When you left for the woods I died. Quite a few times. I wasn't any safer while you were gone. It just made me miss you. But I'm ok because you're here. You need help. So why don't you let us?" Sniffles echo inside Cole's helmet.

The sound of a growl cuts through their conversation. It echoes from the alleyways and rumbles into their chests. Two bright eyes appear amongst the shadow as claws scrape on cobblestone. The hulking great cat shifts into a woman in the sunlight before them, her eyes remaining intense and piercing.

"Cole?" She asks as Cole nods their head. "Follow close," she turns to lead them into the heart of the city. The farther they traveled the more run down the city appeared. Whole buildings were reduced to piles of rubble until there was no rubble left to pile. The flat plains before them are all that remain of the Royal District save for one fortified structure in the center. Even in its current, dilapidated state, Castle Hammerfall was a sight to behold. It rose above the city like a massive anvil with a grand balcony for the Duchess to address her subjects, personally. The sturdy towers that remained carried massive ballista and were encased in a confusing tangle of pipes and steam.

The outer walls are covered in graffiti, depicting hands clenched in massive jaws. The same message is plastered over and over again: "*Will you bite the hand that feeds?*" A shudder runs through Cole's armor. *Such an open call for provocation,* Cole thinks, *they have no idea who will answer that call.* Twenty bodies roamed the fabricated wastelands. Their feet scuffle along the flattened stone. Weapons dragging carelessly behind them.

"They don't look so good, Cole." The Kid says softly.

"No, they don't."

"It's ok," Astrid's not sure if she's telling herself that or The Kid. Her voice shakes like a leaf clinging tightly to a branch in the face of howling, gusting wind. "I'm sure they're just tired."

"Why don't they rest?"

"I don't know, kid. I don't know." Says Astrid. Their guide speaks over her shoulder.

"They can't. They've reached a point where the sleep in-game doesn't carry over, and neither does the food. They are exhausted. Many more of them are in the castle. Some of them don't move at all."

The drawbridge lowers unevenly before them, granting them access over the dry moat. There is no shortage of hatred in the eyes of the Raiders they pass. It's a hatred stoked in fear, folding over itself, over and over again with each tragic loss until the bitterness is strong enough to cut through steel. And while there is no justification for the wanton destruction caused by their hand, Cole can imagine the steps they took to get here.

Past the courtyard and into the grand hall. A battered, red carpet stretches out to meet them like a dirty tongue. At the end of the carpet sits a massive throne, dangling precariously on a hoard of pillaged treasure. The figure seated on the throne raises a hand and the doors close behind them.

"Enter, please! Don't be shy." A crown sits on a collection of robes in a variety of rarities. One of his legs dangles lazily over the throne's arm. His elbow rests on the other arm, cradling a face shrouded in hooded shadow. "Is that Cole? I just got your little love note, what a charmer! Little awkward bringing your friends to our date. Bold move, but I admire the play."

"I don't play like that, Reign. Not anymore."

"You're in a mood, what's wrong? You used to be so much fun!"

"Look around you." Cole gestures around the throne room. "This, all of this is wrong. Your Raiders are sowing chaos in the streets. Many of them can't even stand on their own two feet! We need to put aside our differences and work together."

"Oh, now you want to work together? After radio silence since beta? The gall!"

"What happened to you?"

"The same thing that happened to you!" Reign erupts from his throne. "We both tried so hard to be taken seriously and for what? The dinosaur park opened to the public anyway!!! The only difference between you and me is that you came back to skulk in the shadows. I came back to play the game the way it's meant to be played: by sending a message."

Chapter 26: Boss Fight

"I was so worried about straying out of line. I didn't know what I would lose if I stayed in place."
-Ember

The dungeon floor soars higher and higher above Ember as she falls into The Nothing. Ember's tears float away from her, her descent nowhere near the monster's, or Percy's. With her Tome tucked tight under her arm, she casts the portal spell, trying to fish Percy from the patchwork's grip. It spins back and forth, swinging her just out of the spell's reach, eager to keep its prize. Percy attempts to wiggle free from the creature, but it persists.

Bramble pops out of Percy's pocket, lunging into the creature's many faces, tiny thorn sword in hand. He slashes at the giant with several, annoying cuts, enough for it to refocus on its priorities. It's not pretty, but a final portal spell snatches Percy along with no small portion of the creature's arm, sending her to Ember's height. Together they embrace, clinging to each other tightly.

"You're crazy, why would you jump down for me?" Percy wants to be upset, but she can't help but smile.

"I didn't want to lose you."

"Bramble's still down there, how're we going to get him back?" Ember lets loose a flurry of portals, but none of them catch. Bramble fights on, valiantly, the Hero of Ratlantis pouring his heart and soul into every cut. He squeaks a battle cry and raises his arm above his head, but before he strikes he stops, and so does the patchwork.

"What's going on… Em-… -ber…" Percy stutters in Emma's arms until her gaze is fixed on hers.

"Percy? Stay with me, please!"

"I told you not to stray out of line." Gravity shifts ninety degrees and Emma slams onto her back. The monster, Bramble, Percy, and herself are on a square grid of piercing light. She stands up to the face of Fate, looming over them all, cold, bleak. "You stepped out of line. Abused loophole after loophole. Well, two can play that game."

Their hand waves over the patchwork bringing the creature back to life. Ember reaches for her spellbook, she readies a spell at her fingertips much to Fate's surprise. "You're not supposed to be able to do that here." Fate balks. "That's… cheating!" Their hand slams into the ground setting ripples in the grid.

"Her magic is hers alone, as long as there is strength in my claws." Chance leaps out of Ember's Tome and faces Fate with a cool stare. "Hello, Fate." The giant face leans in to get a closer look at Ember's familiar.

"So this is where you've been hiding. Nine times returned… You changed your name."

"So did you."

"I should have known no mere human could defy me alone."

"Ember can and she has. My darling has bent your laws to her will time and time again. You have no real power over her. You should be terrified."

"Fear is for the Arrivals. I have no use for fear. She is but a drop of water surrounded by my ocean. If she will not serve me then the whole of Galhalla will. Wixley serves me. Bramble serves me. Percy... serves... me!"

"What have you done to Percy!?!" Emma cries out. "You fix her now!" Fate smiles at that.

"Percy's been a personal project of mine for quite some time. One of the original Arrivals. Lost her way. She got stuck in between, damaged, and barely alive. What would you do if you found a stray? Nurse her to health, right? That's what I did. Nursed her to health. I dusted off her user profile, took the pieces I wanted to keep, and boxed them in a vessel of my choosing.

Cutpurse Number Five was nothing before my doing. She had nothing, she was nothing, destined to die at the hands of every would-be hero until I gave her purpose. I wound her up and set her ticking... off to steal secrets and foil plans.

I could do the same to you, Emma. Would you like that? I would have to bang you up a little, but I'd keep a few of the pieces before boxing you away. I could make you a princess or a pirate. And your purpose? Well, I'm open to ideas. Fate is kind, of course. There'll be nothing tying you to your former life or your mismatched body. Reality will be nothing more than a very bad dream." Fate's hand reaches over Emma, their fingers twitching in anticipation only to recoil at the piercing barbs of a well-cast Dice Shard.

"I'd sooner die than become your puppet." Ember spits, angering Fate, their hand shaking in disapproval. Strings materialize, connecting every monster, Bramble, and Percy to Fate's hands. They clench the strings tightly in their fists.

"So be it! You should have given in when you had the chance. Now your love shall be your undoing." Fate takes Percy's string and pulls it taut, raising her to her feet. Ember's eyes grow wide with fear. She takes a step back. The rogue takes a step forward.

"Percy you don't have to do this." Her words fall on deaf ears as the cutpurse stalks her prey. Ember ducks down fast but not fast enough. A throwing knife claims more than a few strands of hair. Ember blinks a portal for the next throwing knife and aims the exit toward Fate. It soars through the air until it enters their vacant eye, swallowed by the void.

The rogue dashes at Ember, dodging Dice Shards left and right like arrows in an alleyway. Ember uses Grease on the grid, but the assassin lunges over it. She glides through the air, her legs tucked tight under her, dagger poised to strike. Ember can't keep her eyes off the dagger, every fiber of her being is screaming at her to pick a spell, any spell, but she remains frozen.

As the dagger pierces Ember's chest, the poor girl's miles away. She's back at the guildhall with Percy, under the covers whispering their hopes and dreams to each other. A fist knocks the wind out of Ember, and she goes down, spewing blood into the void. But to Ember she is back at the temple of the Founding, spilling her heart out to Percy.

"Ember, darling, you have to fight back!" Chance pleads. If she could hear her familiar she makes no indication. The puppet steps slowly toward her, wiping the blood from her blade, Chance leaps up at the assassin, claws out, and yowls. She deftly smacks the familiar aside mid-leap. Ember rises to her knees as her love stands over her, dagger raised for the killing blow. With the fight drained out of her, Ember closes her eyes, waiting for the end to come.

A heartbeat passes. The sound of metal pinging off metal clashes, sending shockwaves into the emptiness. Ember opens her eyes and her heart stops. Percy's dagger is held aloft, jammed in the eyeholes of a well-worn helmet, clenched in the hand of the man standing before her. Though all she can see of him is his back, she knew who he was in an instant. Fate's grin curls to the side.

"This is her, right? This is the girl who's going to help me find my son?"

"That's for her to decide." Fate cackles as they twirl their champion's thread, sending a jolt of energy into her arm so she can wrench her dagger free. It arcs millimeters from Henry's neck. He takes her arm and redirects her momentum away from Ember, sending the assassin careening toward the side. Henry charges at her while she's off balance, tackling her to the ground.

Ember feverishly flips through the pages of her spellbook, trying to find a spell that would stop her dad and her girlfriend from killing each other. A dagger slashes at Henry, the blow connects and then disconnects as Henry rubber bands, leaving the blades to stab at thin air. Two strong arms curl themselves under her, lifting his attacker into the air. He drops the helmet freeing his hands so they can wrap around her head.

"You're just chock full of energy, aren't ya?"

"Let me go!" Percy's voice distorts. Her breath struggles under Henry's grip.

"I've been through hell trying to find my son. If you think I'm gonna step aside and watch some punk snuff out my only chance at finding him, then you're gravely mistaken. All I have to do is squeeze…" Henry readjusts his chokehold. Ember panics. She can feel a scream brewing inside her and a worrying exhale from Percy is all it takes to set it free.

"DAD, STOP!!!" Henry turns to look at Ember. He drops Percy, leaving her gasping on the floor, to walk hesitantly toward this woman.

"What did you call me?"

"… Dad." Henry steps back in disbelief.

"No… no you're not."

"Please, don't hurt her. She's not herself, I… I need her. Please."

"This is another trick," he turns to face Fate, "another one of your tricks! Well, I'm not falling for this one!!! Do you hear me?!? I'm done with your games!!!" Ember grabs a hold of Henry's arm.

"Dad, it's me! I can prove it. Please just listen to me!" He shrugs her off. Ember's eyes pool with tears. Her voice catches in her throat but she pushes through, singing.

"Worry and fright
Won't get you tonight
So long as I'm here

As long as I'm here

The road may be long
But you are so strong
Someday it'll be clear
So wipe off those tears

Even when I'm gone
You'll have this song
I'll be right here
You'll be right here"

"Sarah's lullaby." Henry stares at Ember in disbelief, "... how?" He steps forward only to meet Percy's knife in his back. The blow drains Henry's health bar and prompts the down command, but Percy's dagger pierces through the key command with Fate's empowering thread, shattering it entirely.

"DAD!!!" Ember screams as she watches Henry disappear into the ether. Percy roundhouse kicks her, sending Ember trailing behind her. Disoriented, Ember grabs at anything to steady herself. She pulls herself up and opens her eyes to see the thread of Fate in her hand, connected to Percy who charges at Ember.

She lunges at Ember with a quick slash, but Ember deflects the blow with the puppet's string. Then another blow deflected. Her dagger barely makes a dent into the string as Ember struggles to maintain her grip. Ember tries to tie the rope around her hand but her attacker is quicker, sharper. Her other dagger makes for Ember's fingers, the pain is unbearable but she holds on despite it. Ember kicks one of the blades from her hand, but Percy uses that free hand to grab a hold of her string. Her brow furrows at the contact.

"Stop this!" Fate demands as they raise the string in their hand, pulling Ember and their puppet up from the grid. Ember holds on for dear life, suspended in the air, but she slips slightly, and her grip is slick with blood. She looks down to see Percy suffocating at the end of her rope, her string now a noose, and her hands trying desperately to hold onto Fate's binding.

"Hang in there, Percy, I'm so sorry!" *"Think, think, think! I really hope this works!"* Ember casts two portals on the string clipping Fate's finger. She moves them away from each other and cancels the spell midway, cutting the string and slicing the letters. Fate roars in pain, clutching their fingers. They land on the grid. Percy gasps for air.

Ember realizes what she's done and goes on the offensive. "This is my story, right? Well, it's about time I start making some changes!" She flings portal after portal at Fate, cutting away at them bit by bit. She slices sentences, shaves down paragraphs, and brings Fate down low. A smile curls on her face, and the slight chance that she could do this flutters in her heart.

"You had your fun." The sliver of Fate pants heavily, "but it's time to face your end!" The monster begins its march toward Ember as Fate coughs into the void. Even Bramble follows their command, sword in hand. She sees the hero of Ratlantis and her heart wavers and Percy… Percy stumbles towards her, her pixelated form stuttering, one hand on her dagger and the other on her amulet.

"Chance, what do we do here?" Her familiar's eyes dart between the encroaching onslaught, Ember, and Percy before she realizes what Percy's holding.

"Your portal spell, you need to cast it with that amulet. That necklace is powerful enough to take us far away from here."

"Where would I place the other portal?"

"Nowhere, if you do, they'll know where we're going. Trust me, this time more than ever, it's time to take a chance, darling." Ember readies a portal spell and reaches for the amulet around Percy's neck. Percy's dagger inches closer to Ember stayed only by her conflicting state.

"Fight it, Percy, fight it! We have plans, remember? Movie tickets? Dinner? Dessert?!? You can't leave me when we've only just started!" The monster draws near. Percy reaches for her amulet and yanks the chain free from her neck, her arm primed to throw it at Fate's waiting grasp. Her other hand drops her dagger, grasping at her wrist, struggling against herself as her knife falls through the grid.

"She's mine! You may have severed her thread, but I am her world!" Fate sneers, "she serves me and me alone!" Percy dives down to her knees, cradling her head in her hands.

"I can't… fight them off… Em. They made me."

"Not all of you!"

"Fate's voice is too strong…" Ember kneels next to her, she takes a hand and cups Percy's glitching face. In that touch there is calm. The voices in Percy's head settle and merge into one voice,

Percy's voice. She turns her head to face Fate, her eyes ablaze.

"I… serve… no one." She hands the amulet over to Emma, willingly. Fate's scream is deafening as it ripples into the dark. Their myriad of voices panting in less unison than before. Their letters spill into the void as Ember and Percy vanish from the plane.

"You fools! You belong to me, all of you! You and everyone on this server!!! I will set fire to your stories and only the ashes will remember you!" The shard of Fate wheezes. They retreat into the void, the light of their lettered form rebuilding itself. Their eyes close. "I will find you… No one escapes their Fate. No one!"

The dust settles on a remote hilly dune back on the surface of Galhalla. Ember and Percy cough lungfuls of the grit. Their eyes adjust from being surrounded by nothing to an overwhelming sense of something. Red dust and barren wasteland fill their vision. A dry, heavy heat bears down on them. They dust themselves off and gather their bearings.

"Where are we?" Percy mumbles as she rubs her head.

"Percy? It's you! You're back!!!" Ember lunges at Percy who flinches but ultimately relaxes into Ember's embrace. She looks at Percy's expression and it's raw with pain.

"I did this to you. Oh my god, your dad! Emma, I'm so sorry." Ember shakes her head.

"No, no. You can't blame yourself for that." Ember steps back and looks at Percy then back down at herself. Chance springs from the Tome.

She stretches languidly and rubs up against Ember affectionately.

"You did well, darling. I'm proud of you." Ember pets her head. She looks to Percy, "you too, kitten. I was worried about you."

"Where are we?"

"Somewhere far away from Fate and that's all that matters. They'll need time to regroup after that solid thrashing, but for now, their grasp on this world is not as firm as it was. There's a town not too far from here. I suggest you two find shelter." Chance fizzles away into Ember's Tome. Ember walks toward the town setting footsteps in the clay. She gets to ten paces before she turns back to see Percy hasn't left her spot.

"C'mon, Perc, the town's just over that ridge…"

"What's the point, Em? You heard them. I'm not real. There's no home for me to go back to. I'm not Persephone. I'm not Cutpurse Number Five. I'm just an echo of a person who -did- exist. I can't… Leave." She sinks back down on the dusty clay. "You're better off without me, Em. You don't need another reason to tie you down here. I'll just get in the way." Percy's sniffles cover the sound of Ember's approach. She kneels to lie beside Percy as they stare up into space.

"If it wasn't for you I'd still be at the Sip & Sail. You know that, right? You gave me a reason to leave when I was so content to stay." Ember gently reaches over to tilt her head closer to hers. "I'm not going anywhere without you. Even if I have to sneak you out on a flash drive."

"You're going to need a big one. I don't want to be cramped in a tiny, little thing." Ember laughs until her eyes meet Percy's, suddenly they're quiet enough to hear their hearts beating. "Thank you. I don't know how we're going to leave. But I'm lucky I'm with you."

Percy pulls her in closer. They lean into each other and the two share a kiss. For a moment, they inhabit their very own special reality. Nowhere near as terrifying but just as inescapable. Fate may have dealt a cruel hand, but the only hand Emma cares about right now is Percy's. And she's never letting go.

Chapter 27: New Game Plus

"The Captain's a good man. I hope he finds what he's looking for. Until we meet again, Henry."
-P.A.C.

Henry wakes in the cold darkness of a hospital room. An eerie, dreamlike haze wafts around the room, made only stranger by the modern equipment hooked up to the bed. Sarah's hospital room. Their darkest days were spent in this room. Pacing and waiting for good news that never arrived. Masking the gravity of the situation with board games and daytime television only for time to slip through regardless of the pain they were experiencing. "No. No, no, no… why am I here?"

"You died, Henry." He turns to see the ghostly shade of a woman standing up from a nearby chair. "This is where you go when you die." Henry strains his eyes, focusing on the ghostly pixels.

"Is that you? Or-…"

"It's me. Well, the parts of me that I kept… I-.." Henry reaches out to embrace her only to be met with his arms as they phase through her.

"I… sorry. I didn't think that through."

"No, no, that was sweet." Henry gathers his thoughts and clears his throat. "I'm sorry for what they made you do. I couldn't stop it if I tried."

"That was messed up." The shade nods her head. "Why does this place look like… The hospital?"

"It shapes itself to fit you, into a place you want to get out of. So you can go through that door quicker." She points at the door leading to the rest of the hospital. "But the more you come back, the harder it is to leave."

"What if I don't want to leave?"

"You have to, Henry."

"No, I don't. This world is too much for me. I tried. I honest-to-god tried my best and it keeps kicking me down and changing the rules and I can't keep up! I'm tired."

"So, you're quitting." Henry nods, biting back tears. "Well, I won't allow it."

"What?"

"You heard exactly what I said. I won't allow it. As acting captain of the Dreadnought, I forbid you to forfeit your post. You are to march out of that door and confront whatever this world has to offer you. Am I clear?" Henry tries not to answer. "I said, am I clear?"

"Yes ma'am."

"Good," she smiles, lightly touching his arm "now shove off." Henry's smile is hollow, and although her words reach his ears, he doesn't have faith in the next steps he takes out of that room. Instead of the gaping void staring back at him, his eyes are assaulted with red, dusty dunes and dry winds. A barren village stands before him.

"Hello? Is anyone out here?!?" Henry cups his hands around his mouth to shout into the empty village, pausing once he notices P.A.C.'s bracer on his forearm. Though the bracer comforts him for the briefest of moments the only thing that answers him is the wind. He stands alone surrounded by tents and prefabricated buildings. The sterile white walls he passes by are tarnished by dusty handprints. Blue blades of grass dot the landscape contrasting sharply with the red clay. Tent flaps flicker in the breeze releasing scrolls of paper into the air like pollen.

    He wanders to the center of the town into a building marked 'The Hub.' His eyes strain as he adjusts to the darkness. The room is filled with arcane consoles and monitors, rolled-up schematics, and unfinished blueprints. Henry finds a chair, taking advantage of the shade while he pants from the desert heat. His panting gradually descends into sobs as the emotions he tried so hard to suppress finally catch up to him.

    HenryStevenson is well and truly alone. This is his life now, he reasons. To live the rest of his days until the ghost town claims him. With his end so near and so final his sobs plateau. He sits there, drained and willing to submit himself to a soul-crushing stillness as time seeks to reclaim one lost man.

    Just then a finger stirs. Henry feels himself moving despite his raw state. Unsure of where this energy is coming from he seizes the moment and carries himself step by step. His hand reaches for a piece of paper on a desk. By the fourth discarded pen Henry strikes ink and proceeds to write.

"Dear Ember,

I don't know if this will ever reach you. I don't know where you are. I don't even know where I am right now. All I know is that I'm lost. I'm hanging by a thread. I keep getting tossed around and the one woman who's been patient enough to guide me through this unforgiving nightmare is gone."

Henry wipes new budding tears from his eyes with his free hand.

"I think I'll stay here. Claire's safe, and if you are who I think you are… Well, I'm sure you want nothing to do with me. This tumbling hell is perfect for me. The captain of a crashed ship. If you ever see this please know that I'm sorry… for everything. I know I never said it as much as I should have, but I'm proud of you and I love you.

I remain,

Henry Stevenson"

Henry balls up the letter and tosses it out of the hub with an uneven grunt. He slumps back to his chair, his elbows on his knees and his face in his hands. He sobs through his fingers as the drops hit the floor's metal grating. A notification beeps outside the building but Henry doesn't bother to look up even when a breeze enters the room. Knowing his luck he reasoned it must be another one of this world's colorful denizens ready to take him on another 'grand adventure.' Henry clears his voice, he drags his words through the floor. "Leave me alone. For the love of god, please! No more. No more tricks, no more quests, I'm through!"

"Dad?" He looks up and the anger melts from his face. Ember stands in the doorway holding his uncrumpled note. She stands completely still, her eyes wide with fright. He stands up and steps closer and she steps back. Tears fill her eyes as she looks down at the floor. Henry moves to face her. Up this close familiarity settles in, right down to the freckles.

"Dad, I can explain-" He hugs her as quickly as he can.

"It's you, I thought I lost you!" Ember stands there motionless as tears stream down her cheeks. She reaches her arms around her father and squeezes him. She can't remember the last time he's held her like this. Her tears turn into heaving sobs. "I'm sorry, I'm so sorry! I don't know what came over me. I just wanted to find you so bad. I was going to do terrible things."

"It's ok, Dad... It's ok." She says between sobs. He relaxes his embrace, holding her shoulders to get a better look at her. Henry wipes a tear from her cheek. "God, you look just like her. Your mom." He wipes his face. "Now you got me crying. Is this what you want?" She shakes her head.

"I don't have to worry about how much effort I'm putting into being someone I'm not. It's like everything fits now. I'm so much happier now."

"Why didn't you tell me? Before all of this?"

"I was so afraid you wouldn't listen to me. Like at dinner... I couldn't risk you not listening. Not about this." Henry thinks back to the last meal they shared. He rubs the back of his neck as shame burns in his cheeks. He could feel the argument bubbling in his throat, but he swallowed it down.

"I'm sorry. From now on I will start listening. I promise."

"Thank you… Are you ok with this? …With me?" Henry's brow furrows in concern, she looks so scared. Like a leaf clinging desperately to its branch in the face of a gusting, howling wind. Henry looks at her and can't help but see the same scared kid crying for dad's help in the tangle of Oceanland.

"I wouldn't have been. But things change. I learned a thing or two. I was so scared that I'd never see you again. I'm just glad that you're ok." He clears his throat. "So… 'Ember' huh?" She smiles slightly.

"That's just my username… But I like the name 'Emma.'"

"Alright. Emma. How long did you know?"

"Pickmon." She sniffles.

"You've got to be kidding me! The monster game?" Ember nods her head.

"First time I got to choose." She chuckles through the tears.

"That was when you were in grade school. You've been holding onto this for so long… Tell me everything."

"Well, for starters," Ember clears her throat, "I have a girlfriend… Just hear her out first, ok?" Henry nods as Percy fades into reality looking warily at Henry as she stands by Ember's side.

"Hi. I'm sorry I tried to kill you." Ember tenses as she watches Henry's reaction. "I wasn't exactly myself."

"I'm sorry too. Don't worry, I can relate. Let's start over. I'm Henry."

"Percy." Henry reaches out his hand and Percy accepts it.

"So, are you two happy?" Percy looks at Ember and nods. "Is it alright if I hug you? Promise I won't hurt you." She nods again and Henry picks up Percy in a big bear hug. "I'm not gonna claim I understand everything. I'm clearly out of my depth, but I'm willing to learn." The dagger behind Percy's back clatters to the floor, but Henry laughs it off. "I'm glad my daughter's found someone so eager to protect her. Welcome to the family."

End of Book one.

Emma and her friends will continue their adventures in

Legends of Galhalla 2:
A Death WorseThan Fate

Acknowledgments

To say that this book couldn't be done without the love of my life would be the understatement of a lifetime. My wife is and always has been my biggest supporter, my loudest cheerleader, and my dearest love. Whenever I felt like giving up or calling it early she was there to snap me out of my funk and bring me back to reality. She has helped me find myself in a world hellbent on burying voices. So thank you, Heather, for helping me find my voice and loving me as tirelessly as the day we met. I would not be here if it weren't for you.

To my mom, who told me I could be anything I wanted to be. I'm sorry it took me so long to take those words to heart. Thank you for every conversation we shared just by looking at each other. And every secret lunch we had during the toughest years of our lives.

To the family I was given and the family I have found. I thank you all. The road was long and challenging, but I thank every one of you for the lessons I've learned and the battles we've won together.

To the fantastically brilliant Emma Leavitt who illustrated the cover. Thank you for bringing my characters to life, your talent is beyond measure and your kindness is beyond that.

To the metaphors, the parallels, and every crackpot headcanon that helped me realize who I was. When scraps of representation were far and few in between you were there. I knew I was not alone by glancing at the spaces in between.

    Thank you.

Manufactured by Amazon.ca
Acheson, AB